'I've just been  **Refalo drawled.**

'Have you?' Gillan queried weakly. 'On what?'

'My engagement.'

'Oh. That's nice…isn't it?'

He shook his head.

'Why? You didn't want to be engaged?'

'No.'

'Then break it off.'

He smiled. 'You don't wish to know who I'm engaged to?'

'No. Why would I want to know? I won't *know* her, will I?'

'Won't you?'

Eyes wide, wary, she croaked, 'Who are you engaged to?'

The smile became shark-like. 'You.'

Emma Richmond was born during the war in north Kent when, she says, 'Farms were the norm and motorways non-existent. My childhood was one of warmth and adventure. Amiable and disorganised, I'm married with three daughters, all of whom have fled the nest—probably out of exasperation! The dog stayed, reluctantly. I'm an avid reader, a compulsive writer and a besotted new granny. I love life and my world of dreams, and all I need to make things complete is a housekeeper—like, yesterday!'

Recent titles by the same author:

HAVING IT ALL!
FIRST-TIME FATHER
BEHAVING BADLY!

SECRET WEDDING

BY
EMMA RICHMOND

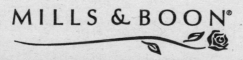

*First published in Great Britain 1997
Harlequin Mills & Boon Limited,
Eton House, 18-24 Paradise Road, Richmond, Surrey TW9 1SR*

© Emma Richmond 1997

ISBN 0 263 80154 3

*Set in Times Roman 10 on 11½ pt.
02-9706-53624 C1*

*Printed and bound in Great Britain
by Mackays of Chatham PLC, Chatham*

CHAPTER ONE

NEVER again, Gillan thought, will I travel on a tourist flight. When I'm rich, I'll always travel by private jet. Not that she was ever likely to be rich, but it was nice to dream. Of average height, brown hair layered short for convenience, Gillan was extraordinarily attractive, with a strong, humorous face, wide grey eyes and a quizzical smile.

She mingled with the rich and famous, but would never grace the fashion magazines that she took photographs for. Not tall enough for elegance, too busy for sophistication, she looked what she was—an amiable, hardworking young woman.

Casually dressed in beige cotton trousers and matching workshirt, she was comfortable and at ease. Rarely intimidated, rarely cross—although, at the moment, abominably weary—she gave a tired smile, and squirmed through the crush at the carousel.

Hitching her camera bag more securely onto her shoulder, she grabbed her suitcase, wrestled it onto the trolley, and thankfully made her way out of the baggage area. A tired official waved her through, and, making a superhuman effort to keep her trolley *straight*, she trundled behind the other weary passengers towards the pick-up point.

As she scanned the waiting faces for a sight of Nerina the impact of cobalt-blue eyes slammed into her like a physical shock, hitched her breath in her throat. He was the most devastating man she thought she had ever seen. Power, was her first conscious thought, Confidence, her second. Tall, dark-haired, distant. A man conscious of his own worth. And she yearned to reach for her camera, capture that image for all time.

He didn't move or look away, merely continued to watch her, an expression of aloof superiority on his face. Aeons passed before she managed to wrench her eyes away, unglue her feet. Feeling a fool, she gave a wry smile, moved on. Nerina must be here *somewhere*, and she would have laughed like a drain if she could have seen Gillan's uncharacteristic behaviour. So would she have done, normally—would have given her quirky smile, waved a hand in apology—but it had been somehow rather difficult to behave normally when confronted by that hypnotic stare.

'Miss Hart?' The voice was deep, flat-sounding—the sort of voice that carefully didn't say all that was being thought. And it was the sort of question that dared you to answer in the negative—and she knew. Knew it would be him.

With an odd, sliding, *peculiar* feeling in her tummy, she slowly turned, stared up into mesmerising blue eyes.

'Refalo,' he stated briefly.

'Pardon?'

'Nerina's brother.'

'Nerina's *brother*?' she exclaimed in shock. 'You *can't* be!' This man didn't look like anyone's brother! This man looked like somebody's *lover*. Her disbelief bordering on panic, she just stared at him.

A small, rather cynical smile playing about his mouth, he queried mildly. 'Nerina didn't tell you of the devastating impact I have on the opposite sex?'

'What?' she demanded weakly.

'But you're quite safe,' he continued smoothly. 'I prefer my women with long hair. Shall we go?' Without waiting for an answer, he took charge of the trolley and walked off.

Quite *safe*? Bemused, confused, she hurried to catch him up, opened her mouth to say—something, and closed it again. He'd probably been joking. Jokes when you were tired invariably fell flat, didn't they? And he must be tired, as she was, if he'd been waiting to meet a plane that was impossibly late.

Aware only of his strong back as she dazedly followed him, feeling isolated in space and time, she fought to pull herself together, gave a distracted smile as he halted beside a small black car and transferred her luggage to the boot. They both reached for the passenger door-handle at the same time, and she drew back as though burned. Her hand still tingling from that brief contact, ears still attuned to the hissing snatch of her own breath, she climbed shakily into the passenger seat.

'You don't look like...' she began haltingly as he climbed in beside her. 'I mean, Nerina said...' Nerina had said—implied—that her brother was *old*, and he wasn't. With a helplessly negative little shake of her head, she tried to absorb the fact that this devastating man was Nerina's brother—and couldn't.

Reading dislike in his brief glance, distaste in his manner, she frowned. 'I'm sorry the plane was late,' she apologised quietly. 'Baggage-handlers' strike.'

'I know,' he said briefly.

Omniscient as well as devastating. Wow. A slight edge creeping into her tone, she persevered, 'Had you been waiting long?'

'No.'

Oh, goody, she thought, and felt the absurd prickle of tears behind her eyes. Tiredness, she assured herself; that was all it was. Reactions, perceptions were all shot to pieces in the early hours of the morning. Well-known fact. Everyone knew that. And she *was* tired. She'd had a punishing work schedule—a week of getting up early, going to bed late. All she had wanted was to go home.

But Nerina had begged her to come for a few days, said she was needed. And because Nerina was so very hard to say no to, she had agreed. She had been promised peace and quiet, a few days to unwind. Unwind? With this man on the scene? But perhaps he wouldn't be on the scene, perhaps had only agreed to pick her up? Obviously reluctantly.

Feeling jaded and weary, nerves jangled, muscles tight, she glanced at him, at a stern profile, at a cheek that invited touch. Refalo Micallef. Founder of the Micallef Corporation. Hotelier and tourist-boat operator—which included running a fully-rigged schooner and a submarine for underwater safaris. He also ran a diving school. And he'd started with just one fishing boat inherited from his father. Impressive. But his sister had never told her of the impact he had on women.

With a sour smile, she asked quietly, 'How is she?'

'Nerina? Fine.'

'The last blood count?'

'Normal.'

'No sign of rogue cells?'

'No. They're cautiously optimistic that the leukaemia won't return.'

'Good. She's in bed?'

'Bed? No. Sicily.'

'*Sicily?*' she exclaimed in astonishment. 'What on earth is she doing in Sicily?'

He hitched one shoulder in a minuscule shrug. A very *irritating* shrug.

Striving for patience, she persisted. 'She invited me to stay for a few days and now she's in *Sicily*?'

'Yes,' he agreed, as though his mind was not fully on what was being said.

Great. Nerina had gone away and left him holding the—baby? Was that what this was all about? Furious with his sister, he was now furious with her for coming? 'I'd better find a hotel...' she began wearily.

His laugh was—discordant. Why?

'I know her offer was impulsive...' she began—and impulse should be genetically removed at birth, she thought disgustedly. 'You didn't know I was coming?' she guessed. 'Didn't want me to come?'

'No,' he agreed quietly.

Deflated, she gave a muffled sigh. 'And brevity is your middle name is it?' He merely glanced at her, his expression unreadable. 'Did she say when she would be back?'

'A few days—three at the most.'

And did she send an apology? Gillan wondered tartly. Say she was very sorry for putting her in this position, with a brother who didn't want her here? 'I'll find a hotel... or go home.'

'No.'

No? Because Nerina wanted her here? And Nerina must not be upset? '*When* did she go?'

'This morning. Yesterday morning,' he corrected himself in that same, quiet, flat voice. 'Because, of course, it's now tomorrow.'

'Yes.'

'Your command of the English language seems a little diffident,' he observed with suspect dryness.

'What? Yes,' she agreed as she reflected on half-finished sentences, daft questions—because of tiredness, confusion, because of you, she wanted to add, and didn't, because, of course, he knew that. He'd told her not five minutes ago of the impact he had on women.

He must surely, therefore, know that he had the power to rob them of thought, of intelligence.

Aggravated, irritated, she leaned back, stared out at the dark sky, at old buildings that looked ghostly by moonlight. Rough roads, open spaces, small towns. She felt the silence in the car to be oppressive as they drove towards Valletta. It had been named for Grand Master Jean de la Vallette, Gillan remembered, and although Malta's history was rich and varied it was mostly associated with the Knights of St John, and the islanders' courage in World War II.

And she shouldn't have come. She had known that, but Nerina's insistence was so very hard to counter. So why wasn't she here? Why rush off to Sicily the moment Gillan was due to arrive?

The car stopped, but it wasn't until he switched off the ignition that she blinked, turned to look at him.

'I can't take the car any further,' he said quietly—mockingly? 'It's only a short walk.'

'Oh, right.'

'Welcome to Malta,' he offered belatedly.

'Thank you,' she murmured with the same off-handedness.

His smile showed faint in the moonlight, but she couldn't see if it was echoed in his eyes.

'I'm sorry,' she offered again, even more helplessly, and hated herself for sounding so meek.

He nodded, unlatched his door and climbed out. Oh, Nerina, Gillan thought despairingly, why are you doing this to me? I'm *tired*. I don't need this hassle, even if your brother *does* look like a Greek god. Or a Maltese one. *Did* the Maltese have ancient gods? She didn't know.

The stars, the moon, the echo of their footsteps brought an intimacy that was laughable as they walked through the quiet streets overhung by intricately wrought balconies. Clumsy on the cobbles beneath her feet, feeling divorced from reality, she felt foolish when he halted and she didn't.

'Miss Hart...'

Turning, she blinked, gave a rueful grimace, and walked back. 'Sorry. Daydreaming.'

'Yes.' Opening the door of the tall, narrow house, he ushered her inside. The clock was just striking four. 'Is there anything you'd like before I show you to your room?'

Punctiliously polite. She wondered what his reaction would be if she asked for a three-course meal, then gave a humourless laugh. He'd probably arrange for one to be delivered. All in that very polite, flat voice, of course. 'No,' she replied. 'Just to sleep.'

Without answering, he led the way upstairs and along to a room, put her belongings tidily inside. 'I hope you'll be comfortable.'

'I'm sure I shall.'

'Your bathroom is through there,' he added, with a nod towards a door recessed beside the wardrobe. 'Goodnight.'

'Goodnight,' she whispered, but he'd already gone. Slumping down on the side of the bed, she stared blankly at nothing, felt her eyelids droop, and roused herself to go and wash, slip into her nightie and climb thankfully between the sheets. Things would look better when she'd had a sleep. Tiredness had heightened her senses, interpreted things wrongly—that's all it was.

But it wasn't, because she was woken with a start at seven-thirty by what sounded like the clattering of tin cans. And she had no more clarity of thought than three and a half hours previously. Hands behind her head, she lay for a moment in the beautiful bedroom and tried to understand something she had laughed about in others.

Instant impact, instant attraction—to a man who was so arrogantly sure of himself—it was frightening.

Another few hours' sleep would have been nice, she thought ruefully, but if she didn't get up, would that be another black mark against her?

Reluctant to face him, she nevertheless showered and dressed in comfortable long shorts and a T-shirt. Her cap of hair still damp, she made her way downstairs. It was a beautiful house—small, and interesting. She vaguely remembered Nerina saying that her brother had bought two houses that backed onto each other. Two front doors, she had laughed, two different addresses.

Searching for the dining room, she entered a short, glassed-in walkway, creating one side of a quadrangle, she saw, and encompassing what, in England, would have been the back garden—or two back gardens, if it was indeed two houses back to back. A tree, a fountain and a lounger casually abandoned on the flagstones. The patch of sky she could see was a bright, unclouded blue.

Hearing the soft pad of footsteps behind her, she tensed, slowly turned, felt the same alarming sensations as earlier.

'Breakfast is this way,' he informed her quietly.

With searching eyes that were kept carefully empty, a face that showed no emotion, she nodded and followed him to the dining room. Coffee and warm rolls had been set out for her.

'Across the passage. We'll talk when you've eaten.' He left as quietly as he'd arrived.

Talk about what? The rules of the house? Letting out a breath which she hadn't been aware she'd been holding, she poured her coffee, eased her dry throat. He was a man who jangled nerves, reproved with a look, made her feel tense and defensive, babble apologies for deeds not even recognised. The sort of man she had never encountered before. The same aura of authority clung to him this morning as it had the night before, and she wanted to go home.

Two cups of coffee and a massacred roll later, she stood, tried for composure, and walked into the room across the passage. He was standing at the window, staring out. A man of enormous power.

He looked as though he'd been out caulking a hull or something. Cream trousers with what looked like a tar stain across one knee, dark blue workshirt, cuffs rolled back to reveal powerful forearms, long-fingered hands, broad shoulders and a well-muscled back, as though he were no stranger to manual labour. A strong neck, an even stronger chin. Stubborn and forthright uncompromising. But then you would have to be uncompromising to amass the fortune that Nerina said he'd amassed.

Well, Gillan hadn't amassed a fortune, but she could be pretty uncompromising when she chose, especially where her own identity was concerned, and that was what she must think of. Her own identity. All else was folly.

'Shall we clear the decks?' she asked, with a brightness that rang false even to herself.

He made a small movement, then turned. Folding his arms across his chest, he stared at her, his blue eyes direct. 'By all means. I'm certainly an advocate of plain speaking.'

'Very well. Nerina lives with you?'

He gave a small nod.

'And she invited me without your consent?'

'Without my knowledge,' he corrected her.

'So I gathered, and yet she said...'

'Yes?' he invited, that small, cynical smile playing about his mouth. 'She said...?'

Ignoring his query, a speculative frown in her eyes, she murmured, 'And she only told you minutes before disappearing off to Sicily?'

He nodded.

'Why?' she wondered musingly. 'She didn't say it would be your house I would be staying in—didn't say very much about you at all, except that you valued your privacy, went...' Went your own way, she mentally completed as she remembered what else Nerina had said. And she could believe that; he looked the sort of man who thought his way was the *only* way.

With a bewildered little shake of her head, she continued, 'She certainly didn't say you wouldn't want me here. In fact, she intimated that you would welcome me with open arms!' With a small, very unamused smile, she added, 'But the arms weren't open, were they?'

'No.'

'So why, knowing what your reaction would be, did she invite me?'

'You really don't know?'

Puzzled, searching a face that gave nothing away, she shook her head.

'Then you had best ask her, hadn't you?' he suggested smoothly. 'When she rings you, as no doubt she will.'

'But I won't be here, will I?' she argued, in tones that were creepingly derisive.

'Won't you?'

'No, I'll be on the next flight out. Going home.'

'And who will tell Nerina?' he asked somewhat drily.

'You will.'

'No,' he denied, and his voice was soft, magnetic.

'But you don't want me here—have made it abundantly clear how you feel.'

'Yes,' he agreed bluntly. No hesitation, no concern for offended sensibilities, and she gave a twisted smile, hastily moved her eyes away from a mouth that was—seductive.

'And I certainly don't wish to stay in a house where I'm not wanted.' With another brief laugh, she murmured, 'She invited me for a little holiday, said—'

'Then you must certainly have a little holiday,' he said in tones that dripped honey. 'On Gozo.'

'What?'

'Gozo. Malta's sister island.'

'I know what Gozo is! I just meant—'

'That you didn't want to go?' So at ease, so in control, he walked across to the roll-top desk in the corner. 'I'll write down the address for you. We have a small villa in Xlendi.'

Following him, being careful not to stand too close, accidentally touch him, feeling helpless and frustrated, she watched him write. '"Shlendi"?' she queried. 'That's how you pronounce it?'

'Mmm. Many of the names are of Semitic origin. Pronunciation could be a problem for you—'

'If I was here long enough,' she interrupted sweetly. 'Which, of course, I won't be.'

'No.'

With a little glance of dislike—never mind the impact he had on her, he certainly wasn't a man she could *like*—she stared at a stack of photographs to one side, idly reached for the top one. 'What are these?'

'Photographs for the promotional brochure—and do you normally examine other people's belongings uninvited?'

'No,' she denied, 'but I'm a photographer, and—'

'Nerina invited you to take some for the brochure.'

'Yes. She said you needed a photographer—which you obviously do,' she added as she looked at them more closely, gave a disparaging grimace. 'Who took these?'

'Unimportant.'

Ignoring his dismissive tone, she fanned the photographs out with one quick sweep of her hand. 'They look like someone's holiday snaps. Boring. Predictable. You want to be different, innovative.'

'Do I?'

'Yes.'

Conscious of his nearness, the steady rise and fall of his chest, she focused desperately on the snaps. 'You don't just want to *attract* tourists, you want to live up to their expectations when they *do* come; you want—'

'A promotional brochure,' he completed for her.

Borrowing a shrug, she continued to separate the photographs and criticised, 'A schooner, a submarine.'

'It's what we do, Miss Hart.'

'I know, but you need to make it different, enticing, exciting—'

'Submarines aren't exciting,' he contradicted her coolly. 'They submerge. And we aren't candidates for the Pulitzer Prize. We aren't entering them in *National Geographic...*'

'I didn't say you were. All I'm saying is that these are—'

'Boring. Yes, you said.'

'And that you should get yourself a decent photographer,' she concluded through her teeth.

'You?' he asked softly.

'Me? After your comments, your behaviour? No.'

And the cynical smile was back. Handing her the piece of paper with the address of the villa on Gozo, he edged her to one side, began to gather up the snaps.

'Why did you have them taken? To obviate the need for me to stay?'

He glanced at her, straightened, continued to square the photographs off in his strong hands. 'I didn't know you were coming, remember? And even if I had, as an attempt to make you leave it would have been a signal failure, wouldn't it?' he asked with a touch of dryness. 'Because you seem to be staying. And so you get your wish. You may take the photographs. Of Gozo.'

'Quickly?' she put in, with a dryness to match his own.

He gave a slow nod, a glint of amusement in his eyes. A very appealing glint. 'If I like them, I will use them. If I don't...'

She shook her head. 'Any snaps I take will be purely for the family album.'

'Sour grapes, Miss Hart? Not very professional.'

Eyes narrowed, she observed softly, 'You're a man very easy to dislike, *Mr* Micallef.'

'Refalo,' he substituted mockingly.

'Mr Micallef,' she argued. 'Friends use first names, and we aren't going to be friends, are we? But I did not *know* that Nerina had hired me without your knowledge.'

'Didn't you?' he derided. 'Didn't know that Nerina wasn't in a position to hire anyone?'

'No. I assumed you must have asked her to ask me.' She might be attracted to him, affected by him, but it was getting a little tiring, always being on the receiving end. Her feelings were purely sensual, not at all based on knowledge of what he was like as a person. To date, that person had been thoroughly dislikable. 'And, all things considered,' she murmured, managing at least to hold his diamond-bright gaze, 'which, of course, include your distrust and dislike, I think it would be best if I went home. Thank you for your—hospitality.'

He gave her a considering look. 'Go to Gozo,' he ordered softly.

'Because your sister will give you grief if I don't?'

'Perhaps.'

'Being as paranoid about your privacy as you are, aren't you afraid that I will discuss your affairs, talk about you?'

'Afraid? No, I'm not afraid, because I doubt you will find anyone on Gozo to talk to me about,' he said drily. 'And I'm not in the least paranoid. However, if it bothers you, you could always sign an affidavit swearing confidentiality.'

'I could,' she agreed. 'Being Nerina's friend doesn't make me *honest*, does it?'

'No, and if you weren't, would signing a piece of paper deter you? And even if it did, do you think Nerina would forgive such arrogance? Your word will be sufficient, Miss Hart.'

'Then you have it. I swear on pain of death not to talk about the Micallef Corporation,' she murmured with marginal sarcasm, 'either now or in the future. I swear not to discuss your private concerns in public. I swear...'

A slow, bland smile stretched his mouth, and she cursed the warmth she knew flooded her cheeks.

'Go take your photographs, Miss Hart.'

Feeling impotent—a feeling she wasn't in the least used to—she continued to stare at him. 'And if I do? You don't intend to interfere?'

'The word is "collaborate",' he argued smoothly. 'And no, I'm sure you work better alone—don't you?'

'Yes.'

He hesitated for a moment, watching her carefully, then finally asked, How fond of my sister are you?'

Surprised, she exclaimed, 'Very fond!'

'Then when she comes back you will confirm that you like to work alone.'

'In case she tries to make you go with me?' she guessed.

'No, in case she wishes to accompany you yourself.'

Puzzled, she queried, 'But you said she was fine now.'

'She is. This has nothing to do with her health, only her—emotions.'

'I don't understand.'

'Then I will explain.'

'Briefly? Or brutally?' she queried nicely. 'You really do dislike me, don't you? And on such short acquaintance too.'

'I dislike being manipulated, and I don't like what you are doing to my sister.' With no hint of emotion, either in voice or stance, he continued, 'Ever since she met you, it's been Gillan this, Gillan that. You have a lifestyle she envies, wants to emulate. And, frankly, I think you're too old for her.'

'Too *old*?' she exclaimed, scandalised. 'I'm twenty-nine!'

'Nearly thirty.'

'All right, nearly thirty,' she agreed miffily. Thirty was all right; she could cope with being thirty. 'I'm not in my dotage!'

He gave an odd smile. 'I didn't say you were, merely that you were too old for Nerina. She's nineteen—a very impressionable nineteen. Because of her illness, she's had very little childhood, very few teenage years to experiment, play games.'

'*Games?*' she asked in astonishment. 'What sort of games?'

'Games that the young play. Flirting, being silly, having fun. I love my sister and I want her to enjoy all the things she should have enjoyed if she hadn't been so ill. And I want her to enjoy all those things with someone her own age, *not* someone who's already played them. She thinks she wants to be like you—sophisticated—'

'I'm not sophisticated,' she protested. 'I'm ordinary.'

'But experienced,' he said softly.

'So?' She glared defiantly.

'So I don't want Nerina to emulate you,' he replied mildly.

'Thanks very much.'

'Look—' he sighed '—I'm probably not explaining this very well—'

'Oh, surely not!' she derided sarcastically. 'You appear to me to be a man who explains things right down to the last crossed T! No margin for error, no room for mistakes...cold, analytical—'

'I want her to be *young!*' he interrupted her.

'I am young!'

'But not silly, not giggly, not—learning. She needs to learn, needs not to have missed out on her youth. If she emulates you, she'll have missed out.'

'So you want me to tell her that I work best alone, that I don't need her help.'

'If you're as fond of her as you say you are, then yes, you will.'

'I *am* fond of her.'

'Yet you have nothing in common. You're ten years older than her.'

'So? You make it sound *unhealthy*, and it isn't! I befriended her, yes—'

'And introduced her to just the sort of people I wish her to avoid.'

'Rubbish!'

'Not rubbish. You took her to a fashion shoot, without my knowledge or consent—'

'*Consent?*' she demanded in astonishment. 'She's not a baby!'

'Yes, Miss Hart, she is! You encouraged her to disobey me, leave me in the hotel worried out of my mind, not knowing where she was—'

'Now hang on a minute—'

'No,' he said coldly. 'You hang on. You introduced her to a lot of unsavoury people—'

'I *introduced* her,' she interrupted furiously, 'to two minor television stars, an agent and three top models. None of whom are *unsavoury*!'

'Aren't they?' he asked with cold disbelief.

'No! And *surely* Nerina didn't tell you that they were? Because that I *won't* believe.'

'No, she didn't. She told me nothing at all.'

'And so you assumed it was a secret! That there was something to hide! No doubt made a great production out of it. Of all the clutch-headed—'

'I beg your pardon?' he asked icily.

'Well, for goodness' sake! You've just finished telling me you want her to play games—'

'Not with people like that.'

'They *aren't* "people like that"!'

'Aren't they? Yet they, and you, encouraged her to stay out half the night—'

'We stayed out until one! We drank soft drinks, talked... I don't *believe* you! There was nothing terrible about it! She wanted to *enjoy* herself, and, the Lord knows, she's had little enough of *that* over the last few years!'

Pushing one hand through her short hair with an exasperated sigh, she continued, wearily, 'And that's why you dislike me, is it? Because I took your sister to a party? Because I took her without your knowledge and consent? Well, I didn't *know* you had no knowledge of it. I didn't *know* you were waiting in the hotel, tearing your hair out.'

'Didn't you?'

'No!'

'Then, for Nerina's sake, I will accept your version of events, but it doesn't alter the fact that I still think you too old for her.'

'Oh, for goodness' sake! We don't live in each other's pockets! We meet occasionally, write to each other. You want me to stop that now, do you?'

'No, but I would certainly prefer it if you didn't fill her head with details of your lifestyle.'

'Lifestyle,' she scoffed. 'I go on photo shoots, and they aren't in the *least* glamorous, let me tell you.'

'They are to Nerina,' he murmured drily. 'Although, if I'm honest, I have to admit that my investigation didn't actually turn up anything horrendous.'

'Investigation?' she demanded in horror. '*What* investigation?' And, even more horrifying, what had he found out? Even *Nerina* didn't know who she really was. Not the whole truth, anyway.

'Something bothers you, Miss Hart?'

'No. Yes. How *dare* you investigate me? Anyone would think I was a criminal! I admit it's an unlikely friendship, but there's nothing *sinister* in it.'

Nothing sinister—just something she wasn't prepared to tell. As far as either of them knew—as far as she hoped they knew—apart from being a photographer, she was a voluntary member of the trust that had set up Nerina's bone-marrow transplant, her only chance of beating the myeloid leukaemia she'd been diagnosed with. It wasn't an outright lie, but it was a sufficient bending of the truth to be called one. She had, in a way, been a voluntary member of the trust. But only in a way.

'Why the frown?'

'Mmm? Nothing,' she denied dismissively. Banishing the frown, she searched a face that gave nothing away. 'So what did you find out?'

'No need to look so alarmed; the investigation wasn't very detailed. Should it have been?' he asked softly.

'No. I've done nothing of which I need be ashamed.'

'Good. All I wanted was a composite of your character, your—integrity. Nerina is a very wealthy young woman.'

'Because of you, because of your generosity to her—and you really can't be too careful nowadays, can you?' she asked tartly. But she was extraordinarily relieved that it hadn't been very detailed, although it hurt that he should think she had befriended his sister because of her wealth. 'You really thought I might be after her money?'

'Or that you pitied her.'

'She doesn't need my pity.'

'No,' he agreed. 'She doesn't.'

'Then there's nothing more to be said, is there?'

'No. Take the ferry tomorrow morning. You won't mind taking the ferry?'

'No,' she replied helplessly.

'Good. They run every hour. I'll let Nerina know where you are.'

'And that's it?'

'Yes, Miss Hart, that's it.' His mouth smiled. His eyes didn't. 'Spend the day as you please. There's a pool in the left-hand wing bordering the courtyard; the fridge is stocked. Help yourself to whatever you might require.'

'You don't have a housekeeper?' she asked in surprise.

'No, not resident anyway. I prefer my—privacy,' he mocked. 'If there's anything you need, get in touch with the office. The numbers are on the reverse of the piece of paper I gave you.' Replacing the photographs on the desk, he stared at her for a moment in silence, and then walked out, quietly closing the door behind him.

So that was how a millionaire behaved. Collapsing into the chair beside the desk, she found that she very badly wanted to kick something. Or someone. Staring blindly at the photographs, she grimaced. A harbour. A few boats bobbing. A happy, smiling tourist face. With one swift, aggressive motion she swept them all onto the floor.

She could refuse, go home; she didn't have to stay. But Nerina had begged her, literally begged. 'Please, please come,' she'd said. 'You can take the photos for the brochure, or just have a little holiday, but you *must* come.' Why? Was she ill—in trouble and didn't like to tell her brother?

But if that were the case, surely she would have been waiting impatiently at the airport, or up early this morning to speak to her? She wouldn't have gone off to *Sicily*! And she must have known the reception Gillan would get from Refalo. It just didn't make sense. Had her brother forced her to go to Sicily? That sounded more likely after his spiel about Gillan's being too old for his sister.

He'd said he loved her, but was it more in the nature of possession? Some brothers were possessive. Not that she would know; she didn't have a brother. And perhaps some of what he had said was true—logical, anyway. Pertinent. She *was* ten years older than Nerina, and in normal circumstances they probably wouldn't have become friends. But the circumstances hadn't been normal, and Nerina was worth helping, or protecting. A sunny, likable girl—and very young for her age. And Refalo, who loved her so very much, wanted her to grow up—whole. Was being *sensible*.

With an inward sigh, she wondered why life had to get so complicated. When she had first embarked on the deception, it had seemed a harmless thing, a simple thing; writing to her, use her as a confidante. All she had ever wanted was to meet the young girl who had been so ill... And she had certainly never expected to meet her brother!

Nerina had said he was old and starchy, but he wasn't. Cold, distant, remote—but certainly not old. And to stay in his house with the chance of bumping into him, of maybe letting something slip that must never be let slip...

She would go to Gozo, she decided on a long sigh. But not to take photographs. She would wait to speak to the younger girl, find out what was going on, and then go home.

Vaguely aware of a phone ringing somewhere, she quickly gathered up the snaps and put them in a neat pile on the desk. After a moment's hesitation, she pulled a piece of paper towards her and began to scribble a note. Propping it in a prominent position, she got to her feet, and had got halfway to the door when it opened. Halting, she stared at Refalo, felt that same odd feeling inside. That leap of attraction.

Casual, at ease, he quite obviously felt nothing, and she gave a wry, self-mocking smile as he propped a shoulder against the doorjamb, folded his arms across his chest. 'I've just been congratulated,' he drawled.

'Have you?' she queried weakly.

'Yes.'

'On what?'

'My engagement.'

'Oh. That's nice.'

'Is it?'

'Well, yes. Isn't it?' she asked in bewilderment.

He stared at her, waited, a rather sardonic glint in his eyes.

'*Isn't* it?' she repeated.

He shook his head.

'Why? You didn't want to be engaged?'

'No.'

'Then break it off.'

He smiled—the sort of smile that made you want to back off very fast.

'Why are you looking at me like that?' she asked warily.

'Don't you know?'

'Of course I don't know!'

'And you don't wish to know who I'm engaged to?'

'No. Why would I want to know? I won't *know* her, will I?'

'Won't you?'

'No! Look, will you just get to the *point*?'

He smiled again, straightened, advanced.

Gillan backed.

'Ask me who I'm engaged to,' he ordered, his voice so very, very soft.

Eyes wide, wary, she croaked, 'Who are you engaged to?'

The smile became shark-like.

'You.'

CHAPTER TWO

'Me?' Gillan squeaked. 'Don't be ridiculous! I've never been engaged in my life!'

'No,' he agreed smoothly.

'And what's that supposed to mean?' she demanded as she fetched up rather painfully against the desk.

'That you're desperate?' he queried, in tones that might have made a mass murderer think twice.

'Desperate? For *you*? Are you mad? I don't even *like* you!'

'Like?' he repeated. 'I don't think like was ever mentioned.'

Eyes wide, wary, she put out her hands in a warding-off gesture. 'Now look here...'

'Yes?' he asked helpfully as he moved her hands aside and stood very, very close in front of her.

With nowhere for her hands to go, she bunched them at her sides. 'You think *I* had something to do with this? That I started a rumour about engagements?'

'Didn't you?'

'No! I came for a holiday!' she said stupidly, as though it were a mantra that would ward off evil. 'And why on earth would I want to be engaged to someone I'd never even met?'

'Why indeed?' Searching her face, he finally gave a small nod. 'Very well. Unless proven otherwise, I will accept your word.'

'Kind of you,' she derided shakily. 'And *who* said we were engaged?'

'Someone,' he murmured unhelpfully. Turning away, he ordered over his shoulder, 'Go to Gozo.'

'Gozo? Now? After *this*?'

Halting, he turned, face impassive. 'Certainly after this. And if anyone asks you will not deny it.'

Braver now that he wasn't standing so close, she demanded, 'Why won't I?'

'Because I said so.'

'And your word is law?'

He smiled again. 'Believe it, Miss Hart,' he said softly. 'Believe it.' Walking out, he closed the door quietly behind him.

With a creaky sigh, as though the breath had been trapped in her lungs for too long, she braced her hands on the desk for support and perched weakly. Engaged? To *him*? Dear God. What sort of a joke was that? And why mustn't she deny it? He couldn't want to be engaged to *her*, for goodness' sake!

With a disbelieving shake of her head, she remained sitting for a few minutes longer. Feeling exhausted, she went slowly up to her room to repack her things. The sooner she was out of this house the better.

Two hours later she was at the ferry terminal with no clear idea of what she had passed through—just a vague impression of untarred roads, no traffic lights, white buildings and a blue sky—no clear idea of *why* she was there and not at the airport booking a flight home, and with the profound hope that no one would ever ask her if she was engaged. *Engaged*, she repeated incredulously to herself. Why would anyone say they were engaged? They didn't even *know* each other.

Her mind on Refalo, with all the things she should have said and hadn't said jammed in her head, she wondered why on earth she was meekly doing as she was told. It wasn't as if she needed the work—she had plenty of commissions back home—and it certainly wasn't like her to give in to dictators.

So why had she? Because Nerina was at the back of all this? And, even if she was, it had nothing to do with *her*! And she couldn't *believe* she'd allowed Refalo Micallef to walk all over her! That man decidedly needed taking down a peg or two! So why *didn't* you take him down a peg, Gillan?

With a scowl, she paid off the cabbie, stared in dismay at the queue, hesitated, then philosophically joined it, face still creased in lines of self-disgust. She wasn't a *child*, for goodness' sake! She could have said *something*!

An hour later, hot, sticky, she made her way up to the crowded deck, found a tiny space and leaned on the rail. The queue for drinks and food looked longer than the queue to get on, and, seeing as the trip only took half an hour, Gillan abandoned thoughts of quenching her thirst until she reached Gozo—and then abandoned them again.

White heat, a brightness that hurt the eyes. Blue, blue sky, an even bluer sea. And noise. An incredible wash of noise. Full of old-world charm, she remembered reading somewhere—more fertile, more picturesque, far more unspoilt than the sister island of Malta, which it possibly was—once you got away from the port. Staring helplessly at the chaos before her, where charm wasn't even *hinted* at, she now knew why Refalo had asked her if she'd mind taking the ferry. Very funny, Refalo.

People with lists. People with *temper*. Tour guides frantically trying to match tourists to buses. People yearning for purpose. One severely stressed driver was climbing frustratedly out of one bus and into another in the frantic search for lost sheep. Another enterprising chap was lining people up along a wall and pinning numbers to their chests, another was actually tearing up his list—and there seemed to be an awful lot of people left over.

'Name?'

Startled, she turned, stared at the fraught-looking young woman behind her and gave a small smile. 'I'm not on your list,' she told her gently. 'I'm—er—independent.'

'Then don't stand in my queue! Sorry. God I hate people.' With a weary sigh, she wandered off.

Yes, Gillan mentally agreed, people could sometimes be exasperating. Moving her suitcase to her other hand, easing the thick strap of her camera bag away from her neck, she began forcing her way through the crush. No one was going to rush forward with offers of assistance, she thought with a rueful smile; everyone was too busy looking after themselves, and if she wanted help she'd have to provide it herself.

Picking her way towards the far end of the port, her attention was caught by a small white car that hurled itself onto the quay and screeched to a halt in a shower of dust. Someone was in a hurry. Idly watching, she saw the driver's door open—and Refalo Micallef emerge. And she felt the same tremor of shock she'd felt previously.

Disgruntled, she wondered if she was destined to get that feeling every damned time she saw him. It didn't bode well for her peace of mind, did it? And it really wasn't fair for one man to have such an impact on women.

But why was he here? Because he didn't trust her not to blab about their supposed engagement? Or hadn't he wanted her to come to Gozo until tomorrow? Why? Because Nerina *was* here and not on Sicily at all?

Eyes narrowed suspiciously, she continued to watch him. Powerful, arrogant, arbitrary. And deceitful?

The car had been driven with aggression, and yet the man who stepped out of it showed nothing more than the bland control he'd displayed earlier. It was impossible to know what someone was thinking when he hid his feelings so successfully. What a pity she seemed so incapable of hiding her own.

'And how did you get here so quickly?' she muttered aloud. 'Power boat?'

'What?'

Swinging round in surprise, she stared at the young girl standing behind her. She wore Doc Marten boots, shredded jeans and a skimpy top that looked none too clean. She had a mop of dark hair, that appeared not to have seen a brush in weeks, and a scowl to deter the bravest. With a vague remembrance of seeing her on the ferry, Gillan gave her a slight smile. 'Sorry, talking to myself.'

'Do you know him?' the girl demanded aggressively, her eyes fixed on Refalo.

'Who?'

'Him!' she retorted impatiently. 'The man by the white car.'

'Refalo? Yes, I know him. Why?'

'Just wondered. He's my father,' she added, with an air of indifference that didn't quite come off.

'Your *father*?' Gillan exclaimed blankly. 'Don't be absurd. He's not married.'

She gave Gillan a look of disgust. 'You don't have to be *married*!'

'I know. I mean . . .' Yes, Gillan, what do you mean? The man had said himself that he had a devastating impact on women! And the natural result of having devastating impacts was—children. No, she mentally denied as she turned a frowning gaze back toward him. Nerina would have said if she'd had a niece. Wouldn't she? 'I didn't know,' she mumbled helplessly. 'I mean, he never said.'

'Well, he wouldn't, would he?'

'Wouldn't he?' she queried weakly. 'Why?'

The girl gave a mirthless smile, began sauntering towards him. 'Because he didn't know.'

'What? *What?*' Grabbing her arm, Gillan hauled her round to face her. 'What do you mean, he didn't know?'

With a little sneer, the girl drawled, 'Dear Mother never bothered to tell him.' Pulling her arm free, she continued on her way.

Didn't bother to tell him? Alarmed, bewildered, Gillan just stood there with her mouth open. Did he know *now*? Judging by the look of cold derision on his strong face, yes, he did.

She hovered, ready to—what? she asked herself exasperatedly. Leap in to defend the young girl? Berate him for not knowing he had a daughter? And then she began to laugh. Weakly, stupidly. First a fiancée, now a daughter, and all in one day. Oh, boy.

'And you shall reap what you shall sow,' she murmured piously to herself as she moved to join them, and was tempted to add, Serve him right. Only, of course, it was the innocent who suffered. Not that the young girl looked entirely *innocent*...

Dazedly shaking her head, she watched him advance on the girl and ask with the supreme indifference that must hide *something*, 'Are you the one responsible for issuing orders for me to meet you?'

'Yes,' she agreed defiantly. 'I'm Francesca—Fran. Your daughter.'

'I don't have a daughter.' Turning to Gillan, he derided, 'And I suppose you're my wife?'

'No, no,' she denied with a sweet smile. 'Still your fiancée.'

Diamond-bright eyes regarded her with distaste.

'You're engaged?' Francesca demanded.

'Yes,' Gillan agreed with a malicious smile for Refalo.

'You never said!' she accused.

'You didn't ask,' Gillan pointed out gently.

'I thought you were with me!'

'I am. Was.'

'Get in the car,' Refalo ordered Francesca, and with a minuscule shrug she did as she was told. Shutting the door on her, he turned back to Gillan. '*With* her?' he asked nastily. 'In what capacity? Keeper? Minder? Hanger-on?'

A hint of warning in her tone, Gillan said softly, 'With her by accident—coincidence. We've only just met. Are barely acquainted. And I—'

'But you'd like the acquaintance to continue?' he interrupted with brutal interest. 'Expect a share in the goodies?'

'No, I—'

'Think yourself lucky I don't prosecute you for abetting a minor,' he interrupted dismissively. Picking up Francesca's bag, he slung it inside, climbed behind the wheel, closed the door and accelerated away. He swerved round a coach, actually made it to the road that led up and away from the port, slammed to a halt, and expertly reversed back to where Gillan was still standing. The passenger door was flung open. 'Get in.'

Gillan got. 'She told you we'd only just met?'

'Yes,' he agreed tersely.

'And do I get an apology?'

'No.'

With a shrug that Francesca might have been proud of, lips slightly pursed, she placed her camera bag carefully on the floor, rested her case on her knees, and reproved him, too quietly for Francesca to hear, ' "Judge not that ye be not judged." '

He turned briefly towards her, stared into grey eyes, and stated flatly, 'Any judgement made on me would be received without fear. I doubt the same could be said of you.'

'Then you would be wrong. I know very little more than I heard at the port.'

His voice as low as hers, he demanded contemptuously, 'But you'd like to know more? Make a nice little article for the gutter press, wouldn't it?'

'I don't work for the gutter press. I'm a freelance photographer, as you very well know.'

'And in my view anyone in the media will sell their soul for an exclusive whether they be photographer or writer. And wasn't it so very convenient for you both to turn up on the same day? On the same ferry?'

'Coincidence,' Gillan said quietly.

'Was it? Or very carefully planned?'

'Don't be absurd.' Turning, she stared back at Fran. 'Are you all right?'

'Why wouldn't I be?' she demanded defiantly.

I don't know, she wanted to say; I don't know anything about what's going on. Yet dramas seemed to follow her around like lost sheep. She'd lost count of the number of bizarre incidents that littered her life. Not that this was bizarre, she supposed, but it was certainly a drama.

Turning back to the front, she stared thoughtfully ahead. She gazed absently at the dusty track, the impressive church that stood above the small harbour, and considered asking about it. She changed her mind. She could, no doubt, get a guidebook. At the moment, she had rather more on her mind than architecture.

Moving slightly, she watched him from the corner of her eye as he set the car moving again. She didn't know him very well, didn't know him at all in fact, only had second-hand information gleaned from his sister and her own judgement based on their brief meeting on Malta. But, *surely*, to have a daughter you didn't know you had suddenly turn up out of the blue in front of someone you thoroughly dislike should produce *some* reaction?

Yet nothing showed on that face, just bland indifference. He must be a damned good actor, she thought disagreeably; no one could be that uncaring. Could they? Was there a very large crack hidden behind that smooth façade? Or did he really accept the turning-up of unknown daughters as though it were commonplace? Perhaps it *was* commonplace.

With a gentle sigh, she continued to watch him, tried to find something—human. The mouth was firm—not tight, not angry—the nose dominant, the eyes unwavering. An extraordinarily attractive man—and one who'd obviously had a devastating impact on Francesca's mother.

Or had he? Alarm she could have understood, or confusion—even anger—but he was behaving as though young women turned up on his doorstep with alarming regularity and he was really rather tired of the parade. Was it because he was a millionaire and this sort of thing was to be expected? Or because he'd sown a great many wild oats?

Her mind crowded with questions, she turned back to the view. This was an island of fishermen and farmers, she remembered absently as she gazed out at the terraced fields, the small dusty villages and always, in the distance, the azure sea—and he was hurtling the little car around as though he were on a racetrack.

So why didn't his manner echo his driving? Weird. Seriously weird. But Fran's aggression could now be accounted for, couldn't it? Frightened at meeting her father, unsure of the reception she was going to get, she'd come out fighting.

Aware of the glance he flicked her, Gillan turned to face him. 'I'm sorry,' she apologised quietly. 'An outsider is the last thing you need at this moment.'

He didn't answer, merely returned his attention to the road, and her aggravation with him returned.

They were nearing the coast again, she saw, and then gave a little cry of delight as they drove above a small inlet.

'Xlendi,' he explained shortly.

She contemplated thanking him for the terse information, then changed her mind; it would probably sound sarcastic, and putting his back up further did not seem like a good idea. 'It's beautiful,' she praised instead.

He didn't answer, merely turned right onto a dusty track, without changing down, and drew up in front of a small white villa. There was no front garden as there would have been in England, just a paved area and a tub of mixed flowers to one side of the front door. He climbed from the car, wrenched open the front and rear doors, and ordered distastefully, 'Inside. Both of you.'

'You don't need me!' Gillan exclaimed hastily, and he stared her into silence.

'I said,' he stated quietly, 'Both of you.' Without waiting to see if they complied, he strode up the short path and flung open the front door.

Fran marched inside, and Gillan reluctantly followed. It was blessedly cool and clean, but almost stark—not the sort of house she would have expected a millionaire to have. Perhaps Gozitans did it differently, didn't flaunt their wealth, show off.

As she blinked to accustom her eyes to the dimness Refalo closed the door behind her, brushed past and halted beside an entry on the left. 'In here.'

It was a long room full of clean, bright colours—whites, greens and blues—soothing and cool, if it hadn't been for the man waiting to interrogate them. Turning back, she stared at him, waited.

He moved his eyes to a defiant Francesca. 'Begin,' he ordered with supreme detachment. 'How old are you?'

'Fourteen,' she muttered.

'And who put you up to this?'

'No one!'

'Then how much do you want?'

'Oh, isn't that just typical?' Fran exclaimed disgustedly. 'Why does everyone always assume I *want* something! I came to see what you were like!'

'Angry is what I'm like,' he retorted flatly. 'And not fool enough to be taken in by some foolish little girl who thinks I might be a passport to wealth.'

'I'm not foolish and I don't want your wealth. You're my father,' she insisted stubbornly. 'Your name is on my birth certificate.'

'I don't care if my name is tattooed on your bottom. I do not have a daughter.'

'How do you know? I bet you've slept with hundreds of women!'

There was a nasty little silence, and Gillan leapt hastily into the breach. 'How long have you known?' she asked quietly.

'A week,' Francesca muttered.

'A *week*?' Gillan exclaimed in astonishment. 'And you just decided on the spur of the moment to come and visit him?'

'Be quiet,' Refalo ordered.

'Why?' she demanded. 'You dragged me into this!' Turning back to Fran, unaware of Refalo's narrowed stare, she continued, 'You didn't write, explain?'

She shrugged, wound a long piece of hair round her finger. 'He's my father, isn't he? It is *allowed* to go and see your father, isn't it?' she asked bitterly.

'If he *is* your father,' Refalo put in, and Gillan gave him a look of irritation. His attitude wasn't helping anybody.

'And are you sure?' she asked gently. 'Really positive?'

'Yes!' Fran hissed. Rummaging in the pocket of her jeans, she withdrew a grubby envelope and thrust it at Gillan.

Slowly opening it, she unfolded the girl's birth certificate, stared at the name of the father, sighed, folded it and opened out the newspaper clipping that was with it. A grainy picture of Refalo stared back. The wording of the article had been raggedly torn away, so she had no idea what it might have said, or why his picture might have been in a newspaper.

'I showed it to Mother,' Francesca muttered. 'She said it was him.'

'Said I was your father?' Refalo queried interestedly.

'Yes.'

'Go on.'

'Go on with what? I found my birth certificate in a drawer!'

'And you asked her?'

'Of course I bloody asked her!'

'Don't swear,' he reproved her automatically. Ignoring the mutinous look, he continued, 'And what did she say?'

'That she hadn't told you! That she hadn't loved you! That I was none of your business! Well, I am!' she stated, giving him a defiant look, 'And I wanted to know what

you were like. If I was like you. She had no right not
to tell me. To let me think I was Tom's. I *hate* Tom!'

Her voice cracking, she swung away, kicked frustratedly at a small table. 'And now they're having their
own baby! "This for the baby,"' she mimicked bitterly,
'"that for the baby. Oh, won't it be nice, Francesca—
a little baby brother or sister?" I hate them!' she added
vehemently. '"Send Francesca back to boarding
school,"' she continued angrily. '"Baby can have her
room…"'

'Ah, no,' Gillan said gently as she put a comforting
arm round her, 'I don't believe that.'

Shrugging off the arm, Fran glared at her. 'What do
you know? I *hate* boarding school!'

'So you ran away?'

'Well, wouldn't you?'

'You're fourteen, Fran—'

'Don't tell me how old I am!' she burst out fiercely.
Her mouth a tight line, fury in her eyes, she added, 'And
I don't know why *you* had to come! It has nothing to
do with you!' With a little sob, she ran out, leaving an
echoing silence behind her.

'Oh, God!' Gillan exclaimed softly. 'Poor little girl.
I'd better go after her.'

'No,' Refalo said quietly as he walked across to the
front window and stared out. 'Leave her be.'

'Don't be so callous!' she reproved him angrily.
'She—'

'I said,' he repeated, with the air of one who expected
to be obeyed and usually was, 'Leave her be. She's
leaning on the railing above the bay. She'll come to no
harm out there.'

'I wasn't talking about *harm*! I was talking about
emotions! Something you clearly know nothing about!'

Not angry, not annoyed by her outburst, he merely stared at her.

With a glare of frustration, she gritted, 'You really are the most...'

'Autocratic?' he asked helpfully.

'Yes. And unkind. She needs comforting.'

'No, Miss Hart,' he denied smoothly. 'She needs leaving alone. Tell me about her.'

'I don't *know* anything about her! I met her five minutes before you did. She asked me if I knew you, I said yes, and that was it!'

'Was it?' he asked sceptically.

'Yes.' With an irritable twitch, she moved away, stared disagreeably at an inoffensive vase. And it's surely understandable she muttered, if she'd only just found out, that she'd want to know if she was like you?'

He gave a twisted smile. 'Unlikely, seeing as I have no daughter.'

'Your name's on the birth certificate.'

'Certificates can be forged.'

'Yes, but surely not by her?' she swung back to exclaim. 'She came on impulse!'

'Did she?'

'You don't believe her?'

'I don't know what I believe!' he stated flatly.

Don't you? she wondered. Staring at his strong back, she eventually asked quietly, 'Why are you so sure? I mean...when you were young, you could have—probably did... Most...' Oh, shut up, Gillan. With a deep sigh, she opened out the birth certificate that Fran had thrust at her. 'Her mother's name is Elaine Dutton. And you are listed as the father.'

'Never heard of her. When was she born?'

'Fourteenth of June.'

'Full term?'

'I don't know,' she replied helplessly. 'How would I know?'

'Then let's assume she was.' His voice clipped, authoritative, like a lawyer, he continued, 'That would make conception the middle of October in the previous year.'

'Yes.'

'Here?'

'What?'

'Here?' he repeated. 'On the island?'

'Oh, for goodness' sake, the certificate only lists the place of birth, not conception. And, before you ask, no, I do not know how she found you, or what her mother said, thought, felt. I'm doing my best!'

'Kind of you,' he praised with humourless irony, then he turned and twitched the certificate out of her hand.

'But if you're not—'

'I'm not,' he said positively.

'Then I'll leave you to sort it out,' she decided in exasperation. 'Find a hotel... Yes,' she insisted when he began to shake his head.

'No,' he said, his attention still fixed on the birth certificate. 'You will stay here.'

'But *why*?'

'To keep an eye on her.'

'But it isn't any of my business,' she protested.

'Isn't it?' he asked, with a rather cynical smile.

'No!'

'Then humour me.'

'Humour you?' she practically shouted. 'Why on earth would I want to humour you?'

He just looked at her, waited. And she sighed and stated quietly, 'Nerina.'

'Yes. Nerina. She's going to ring you, remember? And I will not,' he added grimly, 'have her hurt, worried or upset.'

'And finding out that her precious big brother might have a daughter would do that, would it?'

'Not "might", Miss Hart,' he corrected her. 'I do not have a daughter. And I have no idea whether it would upset her or not, but I don't intend for her to know. And you have a promotional brochure to do, don't you?'

'Do I?' she asked wearily.

'Yes. And it will need your full attention, won't it?'

'I can give it my full attention from a hotel. You could let Nerina know where I am.'

'No, here; it will be easier to collaborate.'

'Interfere,' she muttered.

'Collaborate,' he insisted.

'And Francesca won't think she's being spied on?'

He gave a derisive little nod.

Swinging away, frustrated, irritated, tired, she muttered, 'I was hired—'

'By my sister,' he put in helpfully.

'By your sister,' she gritted. 'I thought it was because I'm innovative, able to give a fresh slant—which apparently turns out to be a load of old nonsense, because she was in no position to hire me, or even invite me. And now... Now I'm not only your fiancée but expected to be Mother Superior to a young, frightened—'

'Manipulative,' he put in smoothly.

'All right, maybe manipulative young lady. But so as she won't suspect spying I am to pretend to be ace photographer for the Micallef Corporation.'

'I thought you *were* an ace photographer. I'm sure Nerina told me you were.'

'Shut up!' she gritted fiercely. 'And, ace or not, it's a job I cannot do if I'm supposed to be supervising a fourteen-year-old girl, or if you're continually breathing down my neck and overriding my innovations just so that you too can keep an eye on Francesca!'

'I have no intention of overriding your innovations,' he argued, in that same smooth tone which was beginning to make her feel very, very violent indeed. 'Neither have I any intention of allowing that young lady to forge any more weapons—which I suspect she might try to do if we are alone in this villa. I cannot leave her here by herself; neither am I prepared to stay here unchaperoned. You were intending to stay for a few days anyway; very little is different.'

'Except I'm to be the chaperon.'

He inclined his head. 'What could be more natural but for my fiancée to look after her?' he derided. 'And when Nerina rings you will say nothing, do nothing—'

'And if you answer the phone? Won't she be surprised to find you here?'

He stared at her, *for ever*, a very thoughtful look in his eyes. 'No,' he denied eventually, 'she won't be in the least surprised.' Indicating the other piece of paper that she was holding, he waited, hand outstretched.

With an irritated gesture she thrust it at him. 'Why won't she be?'

'Ask her.'

With a snort of frustration, she demanded, 'And Francesca? What are you going to do about her?'

'I don't know.'

'She really does think she's your daughter.'

'But at whose instigation?'

'No one's! She just wanted to know if she was *like* you!'

'So you keep saying, but repetition won't make it true. I don't have a child.'

'She isn't a child! And if you value your skin, don't for goodness' sake call her one.'

'Value *my* skin?' he queried slowly as he folded the papers and put them in his pocket. 'Surely the boot is on the other foot?'

'But she *believes* you are her father! She really does believe that! And shouldn't she have those back?'

'No.' With a dismissive gesture, he turned to stare from the window, shoved his hands into the pockets of his cream trousers. His broad back invited touch. A stunning man, arrogant, cynical, sensual—the sort of man who frazzled nerves, drove women to acts of folly. Like Fran's mother?

Her sigh deeper, she persisted, 'If you aren't her father, then why would your name be put on the birth certificate?'

'I don't know.'

'And you don't even remember her? Elaine?'

'I didn't *know* her.'

'Yet she told Fran she'd never loved you, hadn't wanted you to know.'

'Even though she thought me wealthy?' he asked derisively.

'What?'

'The newspaper clipping—it mentioned it.'

'Oh.'

Turning, he glanced at her, gave a cruel smile.

'And you think that makes a difference? It doesn't,' she told him quietly, 'because I'm sure this has nothing whatsoever to do with your wealth.'

'Are you? So why now?'

'What?'

'Why has she suddenly decided to look me up now?' he elaborated with heavy patience.

'Because she said she only found out last week that she wasn't Tom's, because she was unhappy at boarding school.'

'Why?'

'I don't know. She's a teenager. Aren't teenagers always unhappy?'

'Are they? Were you?'

'No,' she replied helplessly. 'But, whether you're her father or not, please, please try to understand what this is doing to her,' she urged earnestly.

'To *her*?' he queried. 'What do you think this is doing to *me*?'

'I don't know, do I?' she asked aggravatedly. 'I doubt anyone ever knows what anything does to you!'

'Then guess. I've had some man on the phone hysterically insisting I do something! What?' he demanded rhetorically. 'Mount a search-and-rescue?'

'When?'

'What?'

'When did he ring?' she demanded, teeth still gritted.

'Does it matter?'

'Yes!' she insisted. It didn't, of course, but she was much too cross actually to make sense.

With a dismissive gesture, he muttered, 'I don't know—half an hour ago, an hour.'

'Tom.'

'What?'

'Maybe it was Tom,' she offered with helpless impatience.

'Whatever. Accusation, recrimination—'

'Why?'

'Why what?' he demanded irritably.

'You said—'

'I know what I said! Do I look as though I suffer from memory loss?'

'No, but—'

'Then don't interrupt. You think I find this *amusing*?'

'No,' she said on a sigh.

Turning away, he resumed his contemplation of the scene outside. 'She looks...'

'Angry.'

'No. A mess.'

'Fashion,' Gillan said wryly.

He gave an irritable grunt.

'You didn't seem very surprised that she was able to find you.'

'No.'

'*I* didn't tell her!'

'No. My secretary did,' he explained neutrally. 'How else would I have known to meet the ferry? She rang me half an hour before it was due to inform me that a young woman had positively demanded I do so.'

'Oh. I thought it a bit odd that you'd come to meet *me*. How did you get here so quickly? Speedboat?'

'No, helicopter.'

'Oh. And does your secretary usually give out such information? I would have thought millionaires would be more hedged about with security.'

'Would you?' he asked indifferently. 'But then the office has instructions to send—anomalies to me.'

'And Fran is definitely an anomaly, isn't she?'

'Yes. As are you.'

'What?'

He just looked at her over his shoulder.

'*I* didn't have anything to do with this!'

'Didn't you?'

'No!'

'You just turned up on the same day, the same ferry...'

'Yes! Coincidence.'

'Rubbish. Those sorts of coincidences I do not buy. Someone planned this.'

'Well, it wasn't me!' With another sigh, wishing he would at least shout at her, show some damned emotion, she asked idly, 'When did the newspaper article come out?'

He gave a twisted smile. 'Last week.'

'Oh.'

'Yes. Another coincidence?'

With a helpless shrug, she stared at his straight back. 'Do you think I might have a drink of water?'

Swinging round, he stared at her. 'What?'

'A drink of water? I couldn't get anything on the ferry; the queue was too long.'

He sighed. 'Tea? Squash? Alcohol?'

'Tea would be nice.'

He nodded, went off to make it, and Gillan collapsed thankfully onto one of the long blue sofas and closed her eyes. She'd had very little sleep, was in dire need of a cooling shower, was confused, bewildered, and way, way out of her depth...

'Here,' he announced abruptly.

Waking with a start, she glared at him, saw the tray he was holding, and mumbled something inarticulate.

He hooked over one of the small tables with his foot and rested the tray across it. A selection of biscuits was arranged on a plate, and she smiled. He didn't smile back, gave no indication at all that he found his domestic abilities at all amusing.

'I'm sorry,' she apologised quietly.

'And if you're lying that's exactly what you will be,' he promised.

'Why on earth would I lie? You can't seriously think I had anything to do with this?'

'Can't I?' Seating himself opposite, leaning forward, forearms across his knees, he examined her, from her soft leather sandals to her short, layered hair. 'You look like an elf.' It didn't sound like a compliment.

'An ageing one?' she queried tartly, and he smiled. Derisively.

'I wasn't in the best of moods. Because of Nerina's interference, I'd had to cancel several appointments and sit up half the night waiting for your flight—'

'You mean you actually have *moods*?' she queried in admiration. 'Something other than ironic detachment? You actually allow your sister to ride roughshod over you?'

'At the moment, yes. Wouldn't you, if she were your sister?'

'Yes,' she agreed helplessly. She already did allow Nerina to ride roughshod over her, and she wasn't any sort of relation. But the bond they did have was—unbreakable, and probably just as powerful as if they were blood relations. 'Did she go to Sicily at your instigation?'

'No.'

'Then why did she go?'

'I suspect because she put out the story of us being engaged.'

'What? But why? Why on earth would she do something like that?'

'At a guess? Someone taunting her, telling her she needed a sister-in-law—someone putting herself forward as the candidate. I'm a much prized—commodity,' he said cynically. 'And perhaps Nerina didn't like her, was angry, frustrated, and so said that she was too late, that I was already engaged.'

'To me.'

'Yes.'

'But you haven't spoken to Nerina.'

'Not yet. I don't, somehow, seem to have had time,' he added with a rare trace of humour.

Not even remotely amused, she gave him a pithy look. 'And I'm not to deny it until you have spoken to her?'

He nodded. 'Don't you think she's had enough to put up with in her short life?'

'Yes, of course,' she agreed quickly.

'And do you think she needs humiliation added to the score? Which there would be if she started the rumour, for whatever reason, and we denied it. Nerina isn't very tough, and becoming a laughing stock would hurt.'

'But *you* don't mind being a laughing stock?'

'My back's broad. And why would I be a laughing stock?' he asked softly, with just the tiniest hint of menace.

'Don't jump to conclusions!' she ordered crossly. 'I merely meant that, A, I don't look like the sort of girl you might become engaged to, and, B, when the engagement ends, people might...'

'Might?'

Having painted herself into a corner, Gillan merely glared.

'Might laugh because the great Refalo Micallef couldn't even hold onto a...' Leaving the sentence hanging, he waited, a small, provocative smile playing about his mouth.

'Photographer,' she supplied, daring him to contradict her. But the word 'unsophisticated' definitely hung in the air. Not that she cared; she didn't *choose* to be sophisticated, to court the attention of millionaires. She could look smart if she wanted to, but for every day she preferred casual.

With an irritable twitch, because none of it mattered, she leaned forward to pour herself a cup of tea. She slanted him a querying look because there was only one cup, and he shook his head.

'What will you do now?'

'Investigate,' he said quietly. 'I shall need her passport.'

'What?'

'Her passport.'

'But why?'

'To ensure that she stays put.'

'Until?'

He gave another mirthless smile. 'Until,' he agreed. Holding out his hand, he waited.

'Well, I don't have it, and it certainly isn't my place to give it to you. I barely know her.'

He gave her a long look, then hooked over Francesca's carrier bag, rummaged briefly, found her passport. Sliding it into his back pocket with the other papers, he returned his attention to Gillan.

'She's to stay here until I return. There are guest rooms upstairs. I'll get someone in to cater for you. I should be back some time tomorrow.'

'From where?'

'From verifying her story and finding out from her mother just what little game she's decided to play. You no longer seem very concerned about your charge.'

'She isn't my charge—and half an hour isn't *nearly* long enough for a protest,' she muttered disagreeably.

He hitched his shoulder indifferently, then leaned back and continued to watch her. 'And you think that was the only reason she came? Because she wanted to know what I was like?'

'Providing we aren't in collusion,' she couldn't resist pointing out, 'yes. I would also hazard a guess that it was greener-grass syndrome. Curiosity. Need. And to punish her mother. I don't think it was reasoned.'

With another odd little twitch, a restless movement, he got to his feet, stared down at her. 'Where's her luggage?'

She nodded towards the carrier bag.

'That's *it*?'

'As far as I know, yes.'

He sighed. 'How did she afford the fare?'

With a look of disgust, she stated, 'I have just finished telling you that I don't know her, don't know anything about her—so how on earth would I know how she afforded the fare?'

There was the sound of footsteps outside, and they both looked towards the door, watched as Francesca sauntered in and slid the door closed behind her. There was a look of defiance on her face, and what might have been tear stains.

'Been having a nice little chat, then, have we?' she sneered rudely.

'Yes,' Refalo answered quietly. 'A chat I should have been having with you.'

She shrugged and continued to stare at him. Watchful and waiting.

'What do you think of Xlendi?'

If she was surprised by a query instead of an accusation, she didn't show it but merely shrugged again. 'Pretty radical. Got any Coke?'

'No. Fresh orange, I think.'

She nodded, sauntered off to look for the kitchen.

'Radical?' he queried.

Gillan managed a smile, then begged earnestly, 'Whatever the rights and wrongs of it, be gentle with her.'

'Do I look like a monster?'

She hesitated, a tempting reply hovering on her tongue, and he gave a smile guaranteed to curl toes. Looking quickly away, she shook her head, and when Fran came back moments later, sipping a glass of orange, he asked her almost gently, 'If your mother didn't want anyone to know, why did she put my name on your birth certificate for anyone to see?'

'I don't know, but you *are* my father. I have photographs.'

'Of me?' he asked in surprise.

'Yes.'

'On you?'

She marched across to her bag, and rummaged in the bottom and produced a white envelope which she thrust at him.

Opening it, he removed the few snaps it contained.

Getting to her feet, Gillan went to peer over his arm. The snaps were all of the same two people—a young man and woman, arms around each other, smiling for the camera. The young man looked very much like Refalo.

'This is your mother?' Refalo asked quietly.

'Yes. With you.'

'No,' he denied gently.

'It is!' Fran insisted. 'How can you say it isn't? Look at them! It *is* you! When you were young!'

He shook his head, looking momentarily helpless. 'It's Nico.'

'Nico?'

'A cousin.'

'But you look—'

'Alike? Yes. I'm sorry.'

'But it's your name on the birth certificate! And Mother *said* it was you!'

'Said it was my name.' Staring at the young girl before him, compassion in his eyes, he added gently, 'He used my name sometimes.'

'But why?' she wailed.

'Because . . . it amused him,' he explained helplessly.

'*Amused* him? He got my mother pregnant and it *amused* him?'

'He didn't know he'd got her pregnant,' he argued. 'You said yourself that she hadn't told him, hadn't loved him.'

Shoulders slumping, face hidden by the wild tangle of dark brown hair, she asked defeatedly, 'So where is he, then? Here?'

'No. I'm sorry, Fran, but he died a long time ago.'

CHAPTER THREE

'DIED?' Fran echoed blankly. 'He's *dead*?'

'Yes.'

'But he *can't* be! I wanted to *see* him!' There was such a wealth of misery in her eyes that Refalo moved towards her, took the orange juice out of her hand, held it out for Gillan to take, along with the snapshots, then folded the unhappy young girl in his arms.

'Come on,' he urged gently. Tucking her against his side, he led her out and upstairs.

Staring after them, Gillan put the juice and photos on the coffee table, remembered her cooling tea, poured herself a fresh cup and carried it across to the French windows. Sliding open the door, gasping at the wave of heat that hit her, she walked out onto the terrace and sat at the wrought-iron table in the shade. A warm breeze ruffled her short hair, but did little to cool her heated skin.

Staring out over the pool, the dusty hills, she sighed. Poor Fran. To come all this way... And was that the way Refalo behaved with his sister—kind, gentle, concerned?

She didn't know how long she sat there—half an hour maybe, maybe longer—until Refalo stepped out beside her. Looking up at him, she arched her brows in query.

'She's asleep,' he said quietly. 'I've given her your room for the time being; I'll get Maria to make you up another one.'

'Maria?'

'She looks after the place.' His face thoughtful, he stared out over the hills.

'Someone should ring her mother,' said Gillan tentatively.

'Already done.'

'I expect she was worried sick.'

'Was she?' he asked bleakly.

Confused, she searched his face and asked, 'Wasn't she?'

'Possibly,' he murmured. 'You probably know more about it than I do, being a journalist.'

'I'm not a journalist,' she denied, cross with him all over again. 'I'm a photographer.'

'Then I doubt you will find a market for any photographs of Francesca.'

'I wasn't intending to! Do I really look the sort of person to trade on a young girl's unhappiness? Don't answer that,' she added hastily.

The small movement his mouth made couldn't really be called a smile.

'Did you tell her about your cousin?'

'I tried. She thinks I lied.'

'About him being dead?'

'No, about him being her father.'

'A blood test would prove it.'

'She doesn't want proof that I'm *not* her father, only proof that I am.'

'Yes,' she sighed. 'And what did her mother say?'

He glanced at her, the same thoughtful look on his face as earlier. 'You're very persistent.'

'I'm *interested*! Concerned!'

He gave a slight shrug. 'Nothing with any degree of lucidity,' he continued distastefully. 'I think she saw an opportunity and grasped it. Admittedly, she didn't know when I rang that Nico had used my name, but it seems rather more than coincidence that no contact was ever made until an article about me came out in the British press.'

'An article which mentioned your wealth?'

'Yes. Puts an entirely different complexion on it, doesn't it?'

'But Fran didn't come for that reason,' she protested. 'She's fourteen!'

'What difference does that make?'

Thinking about some of the fourteen-year-olds she'd read about in the newspapers, she sighed. 'None, I suppose.'

'Then don't make fatuous statements.'

Mouth tight, she said flatly, 'And I was just beginning to feel in charity with you! How did he die?'

'Nico?' he queried absently as he continued to stare out over the hills. 'A diving accident ten years ago.'

'What was he like?'

'A charming philanderer.'

'Who used your name.'

'And anyone else's if he thought he could get away with it. Why don't people *think* before they—?'

'Did you? When you were a young man?'

'I didn't get anyone pregnant, if that's what you mean.'

'To your knowledge,' she said softly.

'To my knowledge,' he agreed flatly. 'Been in that boat, have you? Is that why you're being so—compassionate?'

'No,' she denied, without taking offence. 'And if he was only a cousin you don't really owe her anything, do you?'

'Except compassion?' A brooding expression on his strong face, he continued thoughtfully, 'Shocked to suddenly find she wasn't Tom's, hurting because she felt pushed out by the new baby, she set her feet on a road that promised—excitement? Wealth?' he asked cynically. 'It would make her important, give her something for herself, and, having found what she thought was the answer, she now won't acknowledge that the dream is flawed.'

'I don't know. What *did* her mother say?'

He gave a grim smile. 'Not enough—or perhaps too much. She thinks I should recompense her for my cousin's misdemeanours.'

'Oh, no, I can't believe that!'

'Can't you? What *do* you believe, Miss Hart?'

'I believe, Mr Micallef, that people should be responsible for themselves. I assume your cousin didn't rape her?'

'Nico didn't need to use force. I told you—he was charming.'

'Runs in the family, does it?' she asked waspishly.

'Stick to what you know, Miss Hart,' he reproved her almost absently. 'You aren't very good at fishing.'

Giving up, she reverted to the earlier topic. 'And you really think that's what they want? Money?'

He slanted her a derisive look. 'Don't you?'

She shook her head.

With that cynical smile twisting his mouth, he murmured, 'I have an army of relatives who all think they are entitled to a slice of my pie, an army of cousins and friends of cousins who all have a daughter, a niece or a sister they think I should marry.'

'And is that apart from all the other women who find you devastating,' she queried, 'and who also wish to be your wife?'

'Yes,' he agreed flatly, without a trace of humour or self-mockery. 'And, to add to the list of designing women, I now have a young woman who insists she's my daughter, with a mother who seems to think I owe

her recompense. And a fiancée,' he added as he half
turned to stare at her.

'At your insistence. So what are you going to do?'

There was a small pause, before he offered drily,
'Shoot myself?'

A flare of humour in her eyes, a quirk to her mouth,
she asked softly, 'Made a will, have you?'

Turning to face her fully—a regard which Gillan had
trouble accepting with any degree of equilibrium—he
gave a faint smile. 'I'd better go and let Nico's family
know.'

'His parents are still alive?'

'No—a sister, cousins.'

'A shock for them.'

'Yes.'

'Will they be kind to her?'

'I don't know. God,' he murmured on an explosive
sigh. 'What a frightful mess—' Breaking off, he gave an
amused grunt. 'Too much time spent with George; I'm
even beginning to sound like him. English,' he explained
at her blank look.

'Yes.'

'No, George.' With an irritated shake of his head, he
turned to leave.

'Why did it amuse Nico to use your name?' she asked
quietly, and he halted.

'Oh, not only mine—cousins', friends'... And we
looked like twins,' he murmured softly. 'He was
charming, amusing...'

'Flirtatious?'

'Yes. A delightful rogue. So many girls on a string,
a different name for each to avoid muddle—how on earth
can I tell her...?'

'There might be more than one Francesca?'

'Dear God, don't even think of it.' Eyes distant, he continued to stare ahead. 'And yet, if I don't tell her, someone else will. Not everyone loved him, forgave him his—indiscretions.'

'Like you?' she asked gently. 'You loved him, didn't you?'

'Yes,' he agreed simply, and he walked inside.

With a long sigh, she continued to sit and stare at nothing, then glanced round in surprise when she heard footsteps behind her.

'I thought you were asleep!' she exclaimed.

'Too hot.' Fran shrugged. 'Where's he gone?'

'To make some phone calls. Are you all right?'

'Sure,' she agreed with adopted indifference.

Feeling helpless, Gillan asked gently, 'Didn't you think it through at all, think how he would feel, suddenly confronted by a daughter he didn't know he had?'

'Why should I? *He* didn't think when he slept with my mother. And she's very full of advice on what *I* should do. Don't do this, don't do that...'

'Because she doesn't want the same thing to happen to you,' Gillan pointed out gently. 'And it wasn't—'

'Well, if it did, I'd damn well make sure *my* child knew who its father was! And don't tell me she did it for the best! And don't tell me he isn't my father!' Brushing past Gillan, she sat on the edge of the pool and began to remove her boots.

'He said it was his cousin—'

'Who's conveniently dead!' she spat. Lowering her bare feet into the water, she began to kick them like the child she still was.

'Your jeans will get wet,' Gillan pointed out stupidly.

'So? They'll dry, won't they?'

Staring at the unhappy and aggressive young girl before her, Gillan didn't know what to say.

'He said he'd ring her,' Fran suddenly murmured. 'My mother.'

'Yes. He said.'

'To conspire.'

'Don't be silly. Why on earth would they do that?'

'I don't know, do I? He probably wants to buy her off!'

'Oh, Fran.'

'And you don't need to stay. Now you know I'm *safe*. I'm perfectly capable of looking after myself. And he doesn't seem to want you here! I don't believe you're engaged at all! You don't seem very lover-like!'

Lover-like? Dear God. Ignoring the comment along with the sudden dip her stomach had made, Gillan asked more or less evenly, 'And what happens if he continues to insist that it was his cousin who was your father? He was very adamant that *he* wasn't.'

'Then I'll stay as his cousin. Anyway, he has to admit it; his name's on the birth certificate.'

'That doesn't make it proof that he is your father, just that your mother *thought* he was...' Realising what she had said, what she had implied, she added hastily, 'I didn't mean—don't mean...'

'That my mother was a slut?' Francesca completed for her. 'That she slept around?'

'No! Oh, Fran, you can't *make* him acknowledge you!'

She shrugged. Toying with a long strand of matted hair, she murmured slyly, 'Good-looking, isn't he?'

'Yes,' Gillan agreed helplessly.

'Dreamy,' she added. 'Did you see his eyes?'

'Yes, they're blue.'

'Not just *blue*,' Fran corrected her fiercely, as though it mattered. 'Bright silvery blue—misty. Wish I had eyes like that.'

'Your eyes are very nice as they are,' Gillan commented with a sad smile. 'When you can see them under all that hair, that is.'

'Hair like his.'

Staring at the mop in front of her, then trying to recall if Refalo's dark hair was similar, Gillan gave up. His hair was dark—that was all she remembered; she'd been too busy being captivated by his eyes.

'It's nice here, isn't it?' Fran murmured. She sounded incredibly wistful.

Following her gaze out over the flagstoned terrace, the distant hills, a burnt blue sky, Gillan nodded. 'Yes, very nice.'

'Is he going to let me stay?'

'I don't know—' With an irritated tut as the noisy phut-phut of rotors drowned her out, she stared upwards, then flinched in alarm as a helicopter swept over the roof of the villa, far too low for safety, and hovered not a hundred yards from where they sat, throwing up dust and stones and anything else that wasn't bolted down.

'Oh, neat!' Fran yelled as she squinted upwards.

It wasn't neat at all! It was downright dangerous! Getting to her feet, with the strict intention of telling whoever it was to move to a safer environment, she was totally unprepared for Refalo erupting out of the villa behind her and grabbing her arm. 'Where's your camera case?' he yelled above the noise.

'In the lounge,' she said dazedly, then turned to stare after him in bewilderment as he released her and sprinted inside. He emerged seconds later carrying her camera bag, grabbed her arm again, and began dragging her towards the waiting helicopter.

'Hey!'

CHAPTER FOUR

'Is THERE a film in it?' Refalo shouted above the noise of the rotors.

'Yes, but what are you doing?'

Ignoring her, he thrust her into a seat, buckled her in, scrambled across her, and slid the door firmly shut. Slapping the pilot smartly on the shoulder, he strapped himself in beside her, and they took off.

'Where are we going?'

Tapping his ear, he shook his head and handed Gillan a set of headphones with a small mike attached.

With a tut of exasperation, she settled them firmly over her ears, waited whilst he showed her how to operate them, then repeated her question.

'Mmm?' His attention not on her at all he continued to stare down at the receding land.

'Where are we *going*?' she demanded irritatedly.

'Out to sea. You're about to earn your crust. How low do you need to be for clarity?'

'Clarity of *what*?'

'Shipping.'

'*Shipping?*'

'Will you stop repeating everything?' he ordered crossly. 'Shipping! As in ships! I need you to take some photos of them. *Clear* photos, as many as you can, from as many different angles as you can. And I hope you're as good as you think you are,' he muttered darkly. Still staring down, he suddenly grunted, slapped the pilot on the back and pointed. The pilot nodded, swung the chopper round and began to descend.

Exasperated, curious, Gillan peered from her window at a sparkling blue sea, and a few minutes later, as the angle of the helicopter changed, she saw a beautiful schooner, sails already being hauled in, its bowsprit buried in the side of another craft.

'Is it yours?'

'Yes, and you don't need to shout. Is this low enough?'

'No.' Hastily removing her camera from the case, hesitating only momentarily over which lens to use, she screwed on the 600mm, set the shutter speed, removed the lens cap and shoved it into her breast pocket.

Gasping at the rush of wind as he slid open her door, and feeling decidedly precarious, she stared through the viewfinder. Indicating with her left hand that she wanted to go lower, she altered the focus, and began snapping one picture after another as the pilot flew right round the scene in a slowly descending spiral.

'OK,' she shouted, 'but I don't know how clear they'll be; a moving helicopter is not the most stable base to operate from.' Apart from which, she'd never taken photos from a moving helicopter before—never even been *on* a helicopter before!

He nodded, slid the door closed and indicated to the pilot that they'd finished. Finished spiralling, anyway. The pilot sped them back towards land and hovered above a short stretch of shingle where a small speedboat waited.

'Comino,' Refalo explained. 'Jump out.'

'Jump?' she exclaimed worriedly. 'I'm not a goat!'

Impatient with her slowness, he unbuckled her, removed her headphones, slid back the door and gave her a gentle push.

Clutching her camera and bag to her chest, she jumped, landed in a crouch and stayed put. Refalo jumped, and stood upright.

Feeling like a fool, she slowly straightened, braced herself against the rushing air and kept her face turned away from the flying dust and spray as the helicopter lifted away, leaving them in a pool of relative quiet.

'Now what?' she demanded.

'We inspect the damage from close quarters.' Taking her arm, he hustled her down to where the speedboat waited and helped her in. Before she was properly seated they were off in a shower of spray towards the schooner, where a ladder was flung over the side and, with a push from Refalo on her rear and a tug from a man above, presumably the captain, she was hauled unceremoniously onto the deck.

Tourists crowded the rails; excited chatter like that of a flock of starlings assaulted her ears.

Feeling decidedly disgruntled, she turned to glare at Refalo as he climbed aboard behind her. The speedboat moved off to wait some yards away.

'Is all this rushing really necessary?'

'Yes. Up in the bow.'

With a little tut, she did as she was told.

'I'll brace you.'

'I don't need you to brace me. I can manage by myself,' she said irritably.

'Don't be a fool.' He grasped her firmly against his chest, which was *really* likely to allow concentration on the task at hand, and she removed the used film and put it safely in her pocket, then took a fresh one from the bag that still hung on her shoulder and quickly inserted it. Changing the lens and the setting, she snapped the damage from close quarters, and, because of the haste, because of everything else going on around her—voices, arguments—she barely took in the angry activity on the other boat.

'Do you need to see the damage from the other side?'

Refalo gave an abrupt laugh, and she lowered the camera, turned to look at him, and jerked quickly away because his face was *too* close.

He nodded towards the other boat. 'You think they'll let us board?'

Squashing some really alarming feelings generated by the warmth of his body against hers, she glanced across, took in the angry red face of, presumably, the captain of what looked like a fishing boat, and asked in a voice that even to her own ears sounded strangled. 'Who is he?'

'A confounded nuisance,' he said shortly. Releasing her, Refalo turned to talk to the captain of the schooner at the exact moment that the ship lurched on the swell and, with a grinding, grating noise of splintered wood, the two boats moved apart.

Staggering forward, thrown off balance, frightened for her expensive camera, she put out her free hand to grasp something—anything—missed, and tumbled to hit her head painfully on the brass railing. Forward momentum took her to her knees in a jarring thud barely registered before Refalo hauled her quickly upright.

He turned her, stared into her shocked face, flicked his eyes to her temple, stared over her shoulder, and cursed. Grabbing the camera, he began taking shots of the other boat as, engine rumbling into life, it swung away. Dragged up against him by the camera strap that was still round her neck, her nose practically against his cheek, she gave a strangled yelp, and he lowered the camera, looked at her in astonishment, then smiled.

'Sorry, but it *was* important.' Lowering the camera, he put it tidily against her chest, and the smile changed to a grin.

'You nearly strangled me!' she muttered, unable to hold his gaze.

'Sorry.' With a gentle hand, he touched his fingers to her temple, ignoring her flinch, and showed her the sticky red of blood. 'Small cut. Are you all right?'

'Yes,' she said, without any clear idea of whether she was or not.

'You're quivering,' he observed softly.

'Not surprising after what you've just put me through!' And anyway, his touch was probably enough to make any woman quiver, and the gentle concern in his eyes enough to prompt her into being a fool. 'I'm all right,' she said abruptly. 'I'll put a plaster on it when we get back. We are *going* back?'

'Yes.' He looked amused.

The captain gave her a clean, folded hanky, smiled warmly, and said happily, 'Congratulations.'

Staring at him in bewilderment, she said stupidly, 'For what?'

He looked bewildered, then embarrassed. He glanced at Refalo, and Refalo smiled and leaned forward to drop a swift kiss on her startled mouth.

Moving his lips to her ear, he whispered mockingly, 'Don't flinch; he'll think you don't love me.'

Leaning away from him, she stared at him in shock. 'Smile for the man, Gillan,' he breathed, too softly for anyone else to hear. 'He's congratulating you on your capture of the elusive millionaire.'

Moving her eyes to the captain, she gave a sickly smile. 'I didn't think anyone knew. Thank you.'

Refalo beamed, put a warm arm round her shoulders. And if there hadn't been a boatload of passengers and a bewildered-looking captain she thought she might have pushed him over the side.

'She's shocked from the fall,' Refalo explained, 'and not yet used to our—love. Come, darling.'

Teeth gritted, a smile pasted on her face, she allowed him to lead her to the ladder. Holding the hanky to the cut whilst Refalo had a quick word with the captain, she tried to think of suitable retribution.

'Ready?' Beckoning the small boat to come and take them off, he helped her solicitously down, and then they were speeding across the channel and into the Xlendi inlet. An hour seemed to have been compressed into seconds. Still feeling a bit shaken, *and* cross, she allowed him to assist her up the road towards the villa. His fingers, clasped loosely round her arm, burned.

'Don't sulk,' he ordered softly.

'I'm not.'

'Just think of all the women who yearn to be in your place.'

Glaring at him, she gave him a nice, sweet smile. 'I am.'

He laughed.

'And if you think you're going to kiss me every time someone congratulates us, think again!' she stormed. 'I agreed not to deny our engagement. I did not agree to being mauled.'

'Mauled?' he queried softly.

'Yes, mauled,' she replied staunchly. Refusing to look at him, she walked into the kitchen—where they were confronted by a furious Francesca.

'Thanks a bunch! No one asked me if *I'd* like to go!'

He raised his eyebrows, and Francesca flushed. 'There was an emergency,' he explained quietly. Seating Gillan at the table, he turned to open a cupboard and removed a first-aid kit.

'What happened to her?' Francesca demanded rudely.

'She fell, and *she* has a name. Use it.'

'Why should I? Nobody uses *mine*! Nobody even remembers I'm *here*!'

The first-aid box balanced on one hand, he turned to glance at her. 'You wish to stay for a few days?' he asked her neutrally. 'Then you stay on my terms, not yours. And don't try to manipulate me. It won't work.' Ignoring any comment she might make, he walked to the table.

With an angry flounce, Francesca turned and marched out.

'Maybe I should take her home,' Gillan murmured.

'Yes,' he agreed. 'Maybe you should. Hold still.'

'I can do it!' Gillan exclaimed hastily.

'So can I,' he argued mildly, 'and a great deal more easily.'

Giving in, she closed her eyes whilst he cleaned and covered the cut with an economy of movement that still took far too long for her peace of mind.

'There, that wasn't so bad, was it?' he mocked as he returned the kit to the cupboard.

No, only sheer torture.

'So, what was it all about?'

'A poor hard-done-by fisherman who consistently puts his boat in the path of anything that looks expensive,' he retorted drily.

'But why?'

'Compensation—which is why I wanted immediate pictures, before the hole became miraculously larger.'

'He's done it before?'

'Yes. I'll go and find Maria.'

'Poor Maria,' she muttered. 'Doesn't she mind being summoned every five minutes?'

'No,' he denied blandly, 'she's enjoying the unaccustomed activity. She normally only comes in when I'm out, to restore order.'

With a mental vision of Maria constantly staring from her window waiting for Refalo to go out so that she could rush in and clean, Gillan gave a small smile. He smiled back. An impartial smile, she reflected. Unfortunately.

Seated where he had left her, she cupped her chin in her palms and stared at nothing. Why bother with a smile anyway? First she'd been a nuisance sicked on him by his sister, and then she'd been with Francesca on a blackmail spree. And then he'd kissed her...

Shut *up*, Gillan. It was a kiss, nothing more. You've been kissed before. Yes. But not like that. Not with the same—result.

Wrenching her mind away, she brooded upon his many faults. Arrogant. Smug. So sure of himself. And full of easy charm when he cared to use it, as he had on the boat.

And why *didn't* he have a sophisticated, attractive girlfriend—or a fiancée. Attractive millionaires didn't normally escape the matrimonial net. Net? Who said it was a net? Although, according to his burst of confidence earlier, he was trying everything in his power to do just that. And she could still almost feel the warmth of him against her. The power of him. The scent.

Shut up, Gillan.

She didn't know how long she sat there trying to rationalise something that couldn't be rationalised; it could have been minutes, it could have been an hour. She heard sundry noises issuing from somewhere else in the villa, but couldn't summon up the energy to investigate; no doubt someone would come and get her when lunch was ready. Glancing at her watch, she saw that it was nearly three. No wonder she was hungry.

With a wide yawn, she turned reluctantly when the back door opened and Refalo and Francesca walked in. They looked as though they'd been having words.

'Lunch is ready,' he informed Gillan flatly.

Blowing out a long sigh, she got to her feet, and followed the other two into a beautifully cool dining room. An outside blind had been spread to shut out the bright sunlight.

Maria turned out to be a lady of middle years with wide hips and a wider smile. She made a beeline for Gillan, embraced her warmly, congratulated her, smiled archly at Refalo, patted Francesca kindly on the shoulder, and, obviously happy to be 'doing', bustled about making sure they had everything they needed—enough to drink, eat—until Refalo asked with rather dry humour whether she thought him incapable of looking after his guests.

'Yes,' she agreed. 'I do think that. But it will be good for you to think of others besides yourself.'

'Thank you. You make me sound abominably selfish.'

'You are,' she told him with a grin. 'I will go and make up the other bed.' With a nod and a beam, she took herself off.

'Why do you need another bed?' Francesca asked rudely. 'Don't you sleep together?'

Gillan choked, glared at her, and said firmly, 'No.'

Refalo said nothing. Blandly. And whilst they finished the salad that Maria had prepared he turned his attention to Francesca, tried to engage her in conversation.

Tuning out, Gillan topped up her glass with water and leaned back, staring muzzily at the stripes on the blind. The engagement hadn't been a problem when no one had known! But now people obviously did, and if he thought... No, why would he think that? He didn't want to be involved with her any more than she wanted to be involved with him... Hadn't stopped him kissing her, though, had it? He probably thought she should be grateful.

Feeling muddled, and tired, she sighed, closed her eyes, felt herself begin to drift.

'I think we're losing Miss Hart,' Refalo commented quietly.

'Yeah,' Francesca agreed.

'Yes.'

'What?'

'The word is "yes" not "yeah".'

'So?'

'So use it,' he ordered mildly. 'Pretty girls should use pretty speech.'

'I'm not pretty. Neither is Gillan.'

'I'm not asleep,' Gillan murmured without opening her eyes. 'And if you're intending to talk about me, say something nice.'

There was a long silence.

Puzzled, she slowly lifted her lashes.

'I couldn't think of anything,' he drawled provocatively.

Lips twitching, she gave a little snort of laughter. 'How very ungallant.'

'So I've been told.'

'Numerous times?'

His smile was—deceptive. 'And Francesca *does* have a pretty face.'

'Yes,' Gillan agreed drowsily. 'When you can see it.' Lazily raising her glass, she murmured, 'Cheers.'

'Go to bed,' Refalo ordered. 'Have a siesta. Your room is first at the top of the landing.'

'Can I have a swim?' Francesca asked, in the defiant tone that appeared to be her normal mode of speech and which Gillan wished she would lose.

'Of course. And, if you're intending to sunbathe, I assume you're sensible enough not to get burnt. If you didn't bring any sun cream, I think there's some in your bathroom cabinet. There's also a selection of swimwear in one of the drawers. Something should fit.'

'Belong to your mistress, do they?' she sneered rudely, then presumably remembered that Gillan was his fiancée, and flushed.

'No,' he denied neutrally. 'They're for guests. The house is kept for guests.'

'It isn't yours?'

'In as much as I own the company, I suppose it is, but I don't live here permanently; I just use it from time to time when I'm on Gozo.'

She shrugged, got to her feet and strolled out.

Refalo stared after her thoughtfully.

'Insecurity can make you aggressive,' Gillan began, with no very clear idea of why she was trying to excuse Francesca's abominable behaviour. 'She—' Breaking off, she stared in surprise at the tall, dark-haired woman who strolled in.

She checked at the sight of Gillan, then glanced interrogatively at Refalo.

'Julia,' he greeted her neutrally as he got to his feet. 'Should I say this is a surprise?'

'No,' she denied with a smile as she advanced to greet him. Kissing him on each cheek—kisses that Refalo appeared to bear stoically—she added softly, 'You knew I would come.'

'Did I?'

'Yes. It is a mess, hmm?'

'An inconvenience, certainly. You've seen her?'

'A fleeting glimpse. We passed in the hall.' Glancing at Gillan, she gave her a social smile. 'You must be... Sorry, I don't know your name; I just heard some garbled story about a fiancée—which, of course, is absurd.'

'It isn't in the least absurd,' Refalo put in smoothly. 'Let me introduce you. Gillan—my cousin, Julia, Nico's sister. Julia—Gillan Hart. My—fiancée.'

'I don't believe you,' she said flatly. 'No offence, Miss Hart, but I know my cousin too well.'

'Do you?' Gillan asked softly. With no intention of lying, she left it at that. Getting to her feet, she gave Julia a tired smile. 'Nice to have met you. You'll want to talk, and I need to catch up on my sleep. I didn't get much last night.'

She hadn't intended it as a suggestive comment, but, judging by the expression on Julia's face, that was how she'd interpreted it. About to explain about baggage-handlers' strikes and a delayed flight, to say that her lack of sleep had nothing whatsoever to do with Refalo's ardour, she gave up, shook her head. Let Refalo explain. Hooking up her camera by the strap, she gave a meaningless smile. 'If you'll excuse me.'

'Yes, of course.'

Refalo murmured something to Julia and escorted Gillan upstairs to her room. 'I'll see you later. If I could take the films?'

'Films? Oh, yes, sorry.' Fishing the used one out of her shirt pocket, she handed it to him, and, feeling almost drunk from lack of sleep, rewound the film still in the camera, fumbled the back open and handed it across. 'As I said, I don't know how good they'll be.'

'Losing confidence, Miss Hart?'

'No,' she denied aloofly, 'but my subjects are normally stationary.'

'What subjects?' Francesca demanded as she exited from the next room along.

'I'm a photographer,' Gillan explained.

Francesca shrugged, clearly uninterested. 'And as rich as he is, I suppose. Don't think I didn't see all those travel stickers on your case.'

'Not rich. Comfortable,' Gillan corrected her.

'Which accounts for the confidence,' Refalo murmured almost under his breath.

Did it? Yes, perhaps it did.

'You found everything you need?' he asked Francesca.

Opening the robe she was wearing to show the bikini underneath, she announced rudely, 'Pretty gross, but I dare say it will do. I mean, no one's likely to *see* me, are they?'

With something that might almost have been called a sneer, she began to walk past, and as she reached the head of the stairs he called softly, 'Francesca?'

Halting, she gave an ostentatious sigh. 'What?'

'How did you know I was rich?'

Turning, she gave him a wary look. 'What?'

'You said, and I quote, "as rich as he is." So how did you know I was rich?'

'Gillan told me.' Swinging hastily away, she clattered noisily down the stairs and out of sight.

He looked at Gillan, and she slowly returned her attention to him and shook her head.

'No,' he agreed thoughtfully, then continued, 'Unhappiness I can cope with. Aggression generated by fear I can cope with. Rudeness I will not tolerate. Nor lies.'

'You think her mother told her?'

'Yes, Miss Hart, I think her mother told her.' Lightly tossing the films in his hand, he gave a dismissive nod. 'I'll see you later.'

'And Julia?' she asked after him.

'Julia?'

'Yes. Is the fiction to be maintained?'

'Oh, yes,' he confirmed softly.

'She thinks...'

'That I was responsible for your lack of sleep?' he asked in amusement. 'Yes, I know.'

'And so?'

'And so, nothing.' Lifting a hand, he walked away.

Exasperated, twitchy, she watched him go down, waited until she heard the quiet closing of the dining-room door, then sighed. Hey ho. Perhaps it would be best if they did go home. And why had Julia come? To see firsthand the fruit of her brother's loins? Or her cousin's choice in—lover?

With a little shiver and a tired shake of her head, praying that Julia would be kind to the troubled young girl, she walked into her room. The curtains had been drawn, and with eyes half-closed as she wandered into the cool dimness she lay slowly on the wide bed and closed her eyes.

It was dark when she woke, gone nine, and, feeling rested—grubby and hungry, but rested—she padded into the adjoining bathroom to shower and change. Removing the plaster from her temple, she inspected the small cut, decided it didn't need re-covering, and wandered downstairs.

There was no sign of Francesca or Refalo—perhaps he'd taken her out for the evening—but a cold meal had been left for her in the dining room, courtesy of Maria, or so the little note beside the plate said, and she helped herself.

When she'd finished, and still no sign of anyone, she made herself a cup of coffee in the small kitchen and went to sit on the terrace. When there was still no sign of anyone at gone eleven, she gave a philosophical shrug and returned to her room. She read for a while—the paperback she'd bought at the airport—and with a wry little smile went back to bed. Some chaperon.

When she woke early the following morning, there was *still* no sign of anyone, although her dinner things had been cleared away and breakfast laid in their place. Beginning to feel as though she was on the landbound equivalent of the *Mary Celeste*, she ate her warmed rolls, drank two cups of coffee, and went back to her room to collect her camera. She checked Fran's room, which was empty apart from her scattered belongings, and then took herself off to the village to explore.

There was still no one about when she returned to the villa at lunchtime, and so, after enquiring of an elderly man who was leaning on the railing above the bay, she took the bus into Victoria. It wasn't the wisest of choices in the hottest part of the day, but she still spent a very happy time exploring the market, the little craft shops and the Citadel, a medieval fortified keep with false cupola—a clever optical illusion—and then returned to the villa for a swim, shower and change of clothes.

Dressed in a cool, loose print dress, she wandered into the lounge, and found Refalo standing at the French windows staring out. He turned his head at her entrance, and she looked quickly away, wondering whether she would ever get used to the impact of those bright, inquisitive eyes.

'I thought I'd been abandoned!' she exclaimed brightly.

'But hoped otherwise?' he queried smoothly.

Confused, she murmured, 'Well, yes, of course. Where's Francesca?'

'Around,' he murmured vaguely as he leaned against the doorjamb.

'Covers a multitude of sins.' Feeling rather foolishly awkward, she continued, 'You were both late last night. Go anywhere nice?'

'Here and there.'

Snapping her eyes back to him, slightly goaded by his aloofly casual air, she continued, 'And up bright and early this morning. Odd, because all the teenagers I've ever known have rarely got up before noon!'

'Unless there's an incentive. She made some friends.' Nodding towards the desk beside him, he said, 'Last year's brochure.'

Assuming by that barely informative statement that she was meant to look at it, she walked across and idly picked it up.

'You think you can do better?'

'Hmm? Oh, yes.'

'Then do so.'

'What?' she demanded in surprise.

'Do so. If I like your photos, I'll use them. If I don't, I won't.' Leaning across her, he rummaged briefly in one of the pigeon-holes and produced a pamphlet. 'Use this as your guide. The same places—different angles, interpretation, whatever.'

'How long have I got?'

'A few days.'

Eyeing him slightly mistrustfully, she queried, 'Why?'

He shrugged. 'As you said, the others are boring. And if you're waiting around for Nerina's phone call...'

'You wouldn't like me to get bored?' she asked sweetly.

'No,' he agreed blandly.

'Because the devil might find work for idle hands to do?'

'Something like that, Miss Hart.'

Watching him speculatively for a moment, she finally nodded. 'All right. As you say, I need to wait to speak to Nerina... Unless, of course, you care to give me her phone number in Sicily?'

'She doesn't have one.'

'Of course not. Silly me.' She was beginning to doubt she was even *in* Sicily. 'Do I get a free hand?'

'If that's what you want.'

'And you don't intend to interfere?'

'Collaborate,' he murmured drily.

'Interfere,' she insisted, and he smiled. Looking hastily away from a mouth that generated alarming sensations in the region of her tummy, a mouth that had actually *touched* hers, however briefly, she stared fixedly at the pamphlet he'd handed her.

'Use the white car out front. You can drive?'

'Yes, I can drive.'

'Then drive carefully. Be alert at junctions. We have no traffic lights. Toot and cross cautiously. Tourists can be the very devil in hired cars. There are eleven villages; Victoria is the capital, commonly known as Rabat—'

'Yes, why *is* that?' she asked. It was something that had been puzzling her all day. Every time she'd asked, all she'd ever got in reply was a whimsical smile.

'It was changed from Rabat in honour of Queen Victoria. So officially it's Victoria—'

'But the locals like to stick with tradition?'

'Something like that.'

Returning her gaze to last year's brochure, because it was a great deal easier than looking at him, and seeing the small photograph of him on the inside page, she quickly read the caption. 'Oh!' she exclaimed as though she were surprised. 'You're Gozitan!'

'Yes. There's a map in one of the drawers. Rummage at will. You've eaten?'

Was he hoping she had? 'No,' she replied.

'Then I'll get Maria to lay you something in the dining room. *Bon appetit.*' With an odd little dip of his head, he strolled out, and left Gillan feeling—bemused. And stupid.

Why did he always manage to make her feel such a no-brain? She'd had more informative conversations with plants! He was obviously a man who didn't like being asked questions. Because she was a photographer, and photographers were like journalists?

With a little shrug, she collapsed into the desk chair, opened the pamphlet and began to read about Gozo—about its history, its people—and gave a rueful smile as she came to the bit about the Maltese regarding the Gozitans as simple peasants. Refalo, a simple peasant? She didn't think so.

Then she laughed aloud as she read that 'In reality, it takes only one Gozitan to put ten Maltese in his pocket.' She didn't know any Maltese people, and only one Gozitan—Refalo—but if they were all like him it could certainly be true.

Finding the map in the top drawer, she marked out the sites mentioned in the pamphlet, and left it ready for the morning. Feeling abandoned, she got up to find Maria and her solitary dinner.

The next morning, with still no sign of Francesca— although her bed had been slept in, which was a relief— and with no expectation of seeing Refalo, Gillan ate a solitary breakfast and, armed with her camera and the map, set out to explore.

With a rough idea in her mind of what she wanted to do, what effects she was aiming for, she got on with her work. Hopefully, Nerina would ring this evening, and if she could manage to get the bulk of the photography done today, and finish the rest tomorrow, then she could go home. To sanity.

She visited the megalithic temple of Ggantija, the harbour, Fort Chambray and Ramla, the legendary landing place of Ulysses, who, it was said, had been shipwrecked on Gozo and kept captive by the nymph, Calypso, for seven years. What it didn't say, and what no one had warned her about, was that the cave where he had supposedly been kept was only reached by the agile and venturesome.

With scraped knees and elbows, hot, grubby and sweaty, she returned to the villa for a shower, then a long, leisurely swim in the pool. Alone. She saw Maria, but pumping Maria for information about her host or reluctant charge was like pumping rock. Nerina hadn't rung. With no desire to sit around waiting for someone to show up, she decided to hire out one of the small boats for the shots she needed to take from the sea.

Assuring the concerned boatman that she could handle the craft, and with instructions on what she must or must not do ringing in her ears, she puttered out of the bay. Hugging the coast, she motored round to Fungus Rock, then anchored off the Azure Window, a natural marvel in the south-west of the island, and waited for the sun to sink low enough to give her the shot she wanted.

Patient when she needed to be, experienced enough to know what would work and what wouldn't, she waited. And with the gentle breeze ruffling her hair, the gentle swell soothing her, feeling more happy and contented than she had felt in years, Refalo pushed to the back of her mind, she found the sinking sun a gentle benediction.

There! She took six photographs, then quickly manoeuvred the small craft round to enable her to get both the Azure Window and Fungus Rock into one shot.

Waiting patiently until long shadows gave her the contrast she needed, she finished the film.

With a sigh of satisfaction for work well done, she carefully removed the lens and fitted it into her bag. Wiping away any spray that might have caught her camera, she replaced the lens cap and put everything back in her bag.

And suddenly it was full dark. The transition from light to dark seemed too swift to comprehend, and she realised too late that, with most of the shoreline unpopulated, there would be few lights, if any, to show her where the land was. Still, it was only about two miles, and surely the wash of breakers would show her any hazards in advance? Once round Wardija Point, she would probably be able to see the lights from Xlendi.

Although the man who'd hired her the boat would probably be getting a bit alarmed. She had promised him she would be back before it got dark. Hand on the starter cord, she jumped in alarm when sound and light hit her both at once.

Squinting, one hand up to shield her eyes, the familiar phut-phut of the helicopter reassured her. There was a splash nearby and, seconds later, as the helicopter wheeled away, strong hands grasped the hull—and Refalo climbed aboard. Odd, how she knew it was him. Even in the dark.

'Am I not paying enough attention to you, Miss Hart?' he queried coldly. 'Thought you'd create a little drama?'

Astonished, she queried weakly, 'What?'

A torch was switched on and she looked quickly away from the bright glare.

'Yes, you do well to look away,' he castigated her in the mild, distasteful tone that always made her want to hit him. 'Do you have *any* idea how much trouble such irresponsibility causes?'

'I *wasn't* being—'

'Weren't you?'

'No! And will you please let me finish a sentence before you leap in with another? I was perfectly all right!'

'Were you? And everyone knew that, did they? The villagers, the boatman, Maria?'

'No...well...' she mumbled. 'I didn't mean to be this late. I'm sorry.'

'And that makes it all right, does it?'

'No. I—'

'Do you have any running lights? Flares?' he continued remorselessly.

'No, I—'

Do you know the coastline? The hazards? The currents?'

'No.'

'No,' he agreed scathingly. 'And do you know how many people die through such sheer, unthinking folly? You told Cesare you were going to the end of the inlet and would be back before dark. A patent lie. People could have been put at risk searching for you in all the wrong places—'

'All right!' she broke in crossly. 'I'm sorry!' I didn't mean to worry anyone. And if you're angry, would you please just shout at me? I find it so much easier to cope with!'

'I never shout.'

'No,' she muttered disparagingly. 'Just quietly brood. I've said I'm sorry. Twice,' she muttered under her breath.

'So you did,' he agreed pithily. 'You could have *died* out here. What on earth were you *doing* until this time? You can't take photographs in the dark!'

Well, you could, but... 'Sunset,' she murmured.

'Sunset,' he repeated flatly. 'And after the sun sets it gets dark. You'd planned for that, had you? Or are you really so stupid that you thought you could navigate back in pitch-darkness, having been on the island for three days? You know none of the landmarks—'

Breaking off, he muttered something she didn't catch. Hair still dripping, causing fascinating little rivulets down his naked chest, powerful legs astride, his cotton trousers clinging wetly, feet bare, he glared down at her bent head.

'Look at me!' he ordered, and she obediently raised her head, mutinously stared into glittering pale eyes.

'Don't you *ever*— Oh, get in the bow,' he ordered tiredly. 'Carefully,' he added in unnecessary warning.

Crawling past him, past a wet, naked chest, she settled herself in the bow, her back to him. He said nothing else, merely settled himself in the stern seat and fired the engine into noisy life.

Feeling like a scolded child, she kept quiet.

It didn't take long to get back to Xlendi. He moored beside the rock face, tied up, and with an abrupt movement of his hand bade her wait until he'd climbed up to the little promenade fashioned into the cliff. Leaning back, he indicated irritably for her to give him her hand. As he hauled her up after him she stumbled, fell against his chest, and his arm automatically clamped her steady.

Face squashed uncomfortably against damp skin, hands limp by her sides, feeling almost faint at such close contact, she took a cautious breath, opened her mouth to speak, say something—anything—and found that the small movement dragged her lips across his nipple. Her shudder only half completed, he moved her away so fast that if he hadn't been holding her shoulders she would have fallen.

'It isn't *real*, Miss Hart!' he said scathingly.

'What?' Staring up at him, eyes wide, she repeated blankly, 'What?'

'Our engagement.'

'I never said it was!'

Then don't "accidentally" slip against me!'

'I didn't!'

He gave a mirthless smile. 'Didn't you?'

'No.'

'I don't believe you. You think you would like to be held by me, kissed by me, made love to by me? Then let me disabuse you.'

With a movement too swift to comprehend, he caught the back of her neck in an iron fist, lowered his head and kissed her. It was a hard, brutal assault that bruised the soft tissue of her lips against her teeth. The hand that still held the torch was pressed painfully into her back, and the iron clamp on her neck paralysed her.

With an angry jerk, he released her.

Numb, disbelieving, breathing heavily, eyes wide with the sheen of pain-wrought tears, she just stared at him—did not hear the soft tap of footsteps on the road above, did not hear them halt. She saw him glance up, but before she could recover her wits, run, berate him, she was once more in his arms—but quite unprepared for the searing kiss that robbed her of reason, scattered any wits she had left. A kiss as unlike the other as pleasure was unlike pain.

CHAPTER FIVE

AND then it was over, and Refalo released her, stepped back.

'My apologies,' he said stiffly. 'That was unforgivable.'

Her emotions in turmoil, trying so very hard to steady them, Gillan stared up at him, managed thickly, 'Why was it?'

'Because it was for the wrong reasons.'

'And what *were* the reasons?'

'The woman above you.'

Bewildered, as if in a trance, she looked up. 'There's no one there,' she said unsteadily.

'No. She's gone.'

Staring at him, she managed more or less sensibly, 'You kissed me because someone was watching? A woman? Someone who'd heard of our engagement?'

'Yes.'

'But you kissed me before, on the schooner, and you didn't apologise.'

'No.'

'So why the difference?'

'In the kiss, or the apology?'

'Don't play games,' she stormed raggedly. 'Please, do not play games! I'm not in the mood.'

'No,' he agreed quietly. 'Let's get you inside. We can talk about it there. Have you eaten?'

'I had some lunch,' she said stiffly. It was amazing that her voice even worked, she thought dazedly.

If he hadn't kissed her again, had left her with that first hard, brutal impression, she could have hated him, been justifiably angry. But he hadn't, and she didn't know how to be angry any more.

Feeling unutterably distressed, she allowed him to lead her up the remaining steps to the road, and then across it and towards the villa. Their footsteps crunched loudly on the gravel; the torch beam wavered wildly as though frightened of attack.

Disorientated, her mind was stuck in the rut that was Refalo. That initial meeting with him, that impact of awareness had been a silly thing, a fun thing—a flare of attraction that was normal, ordinary. She hadn't yearned for his body, or wanted him to fall in love with her; it had just been—attraction. But now...

Eyes troubled, unseeing, she caught his arm, halted him. 'Why did you think I was creating drama?'

'It's not important,' he replied flatly. 'Leave it.'

'No. You said... As though... Damn it, Refalo, you can't just make statements and walk off!'

'Can't I?' he asked quietly. 'Maria's waiting.'

With a tut of frustration, she turned in through the gate, giving Maria a lame smile.

'You are safe!' she exclaimed. 'Thank the good Lord. We have been very worried. 'Come inside.' With a beam of relief, she glanced at Refalo, and he gave a small nod. Confirmation that she was safe, unharmed? But she wasn't.

'I'm sorry,' she apologised to the older woman, and her words sounded hollow, echoey. 'I didn't mean to worry anyone.'

'Is no longer important. You are safe. I will heat your meal.' Bustling back inside, she left them to follow her.

'Go and have something to eat,' Refalo ordered quietly. 'I'll go and get out of these wet things.'

She nodded, and, grateful to be alone, walked into the dining room. Within minutes Maria was back with lasagne, hot coffee and warmed rolls.

'Anything else I can do?'

'No, thank you.'

'Then I will say goodnight.' With a warm smile, a gentle pat on the shoulder, she reproved her gently. 'Don't look so worried.'

Worried? She was more than worried. She was aghast. Managing a smile, she shook her head. 'Goodnight, Maria.'

Toying with her meal, no longer very hungry, she eventually pushed it aside and poured her coffee. Elbows on the table, gaze distant, she sipped the hot brew, tried to mock herself. A kiss that was indescribable—a warm fire on a cold night, sunlight on water. Over before it had properly begun, but it had felt like—coming home.

Don't think of it, she scolded herself; think of the first kiss, concentrate on that, on the harshness of it, the brutality. Running her tongue gingerly along the inside of her lips, she felt the puffiness, tasted the faint trace of blood. Focus on that, she told herself; don't think of the other one.

Hearing his light footsteps on the stairs, she roused herself, tried to regulate her skittering heartbeat, tried to look normal. She doubted if she succeeded. Keeping her eyes very firmly away from where she knew he stood, muscles tight, she stared into her coffee.

He didn't speak. Just stood there.

Unable to bear the silence, the—fraughtness, she queried, 'Francesca's asleep?' And her voice sounded thick, unnatural. 'She obviously wasn't worried,' she babbled. 'But then why should she be?'

When he didn't answer, didn't move, just remained standing in the doorway behind her, she glanced warily round, then as quickly away, but the expression on his face had been ... And she realised something she should have realised earlier. Fool, Gillan. Where have your brains been since you met this man? 'She isn't here, is she?' she stated quietly.

Face expressionless, he walked into her line of vision and finally shook his head. 'No.'

'And how long hasn't she been here?'

'Since the day you arrived. You haven't eaten your meal.'

'No.' Still searching the surface of her coffee as though all answers might be there, she murmured, 'But you said...'

'Yes.' Halting at the table, he poured himself a cup of coffee, added cream, slowly stirred it in, eyes on his task.

Glancing quickly up, mind scurrying uselessly, she gave a funny little sigh. 'Where is she? In England? You sent her home?'

'No, with Julia. Malta. She can tell her more about Nico than I ever could. She has photographs, memories...'

'And Fran didn't mind going?'

'No. It will enable her to find out about her father.'

'Will they be kind to her?'

He gave a mirthless smile. 'Oh, yes.'

'Why did you say it like that?'

He looked at her, held her gaze trapped for endless seconds. 'I have money, Miss Hart. A favour done,' he murmured cynically.

'*Everyone* can't be after your money! *Someone* must like you for yourself!'

'Must they? Do you?' he asked silkily.

Ignoring him, shying away like a frightened horse, she demanded, 'Why didn't you tell me?'

Eyes down, he continued to stir his coffee. 'Because, had you known, you might have left. Mightn't you?' he queried as he finally looked at her, his eyes bright, probing, disturbing.

'Possibly.' No possibility about it.

'So I didn't tell you.'

'Why?'

'Because I wanted you to stay.'

'Because of Nerina,' she stated flatly. 'Because we're "engaged".'

'Yes.' Putting his spoon tidily in the saucer, he raised the cup to his mouth. A mouth that touched hers. For all the wrong reasons. 'Have you ever been in love, Gillan?'

'What? What does that have to do with anything?' she queried weakly, but her heart was beating too fast, and her hands felt clammy.

'Have you?' he persisted.

With a feeling almost of hysteria she wondered if he was going to proposition her! But no, he didn't like women with short hair, did he? Perhaps his code of ethics meant that he had to recompense her for that kiss. Perhaps he was afraid she would think he'd fallen in love with her and needed to set the record straight.

'When I was thirteen,' she muttered flippantly, 'the butcher's boy featured largely. I think.'

'You think it was the butcher's boy? Or think you were thirteen?' he queried.

'Thirteen.' And don't be smart with me, she told him, silently savage. 'And then there was a rather gorgeous tutor at university that I lusted after,' she continued sarcastically, and with a bitterness that astonished even her. 'And I have been kissed before, if that's what this is all about. Even unsophisticated girls get propositioned, you know.'

'And did you take up any of these propositions?' he asked, in that same quiet voice.

'Mind your own business. And you really mustn't think that I don't know the difference between expediency and lust,' she continued with the same bitterness. 'I might be ordinary but I have had some experience. I also read a lot!'

'Ordinary?' he queried, looking up. 'You aren't in the least ordinary.'

'Why, thank you. How nice of you to say so!'

His eyes widened, as though he was surprised by her outburst, and then he frowned. 'We seem, somehow, to be at cross purposes.'

'Do we? How odd. I could have sworn you were just about to explain that your kisses hadn't been meant personally.'

'No,' he denied, that flicker of surprise still in his eyes. 'One I thought deserved, and the other I've already apologised for.'

Wanting to throw something, she borrowed one of his mirthless smiles. 'So what's going on? Why keep asking me about love affairs?'

He gave a faint smile. 'I didn't, and you sound like Francesca.'

'I *feel* like Francesca!' With a little glare that she was unable to maintain, she stared down into her coffee.

'So much for leading up to it slowly,' he murmured wryly. 'I asked about being in love because I wondered, idly, whether you would be convincing as a lover.'

Choking on her coffee, she spluttered, 'What? *What?*'

A little dimple appeared in one cheek, fascinating her, and she had to forcibly wrench her attention back to what he was saying.

'People keep commenting on the fact that we don't seem very—lover-like.'

'Really,' she muttered with intended indifference.

'Yes. And when Julia was here, and she got the wrong end of the stick... Not surprising,' he added with another wry smile. 'Julia often gets hold of the wrong end of the stick.'

'Poor Julia,' she commented pithily. 'Perhaps if you tried explaining things to her—'

'Waste of time. Julia believes what she wants to believe.'

'She didn't believe in our engagement,' she pointed out.

'No—mostly because she didn't *want* to believe it. But just in case it was real...'

'She needed to come and see for herself?'

'Something like that. She believes we're *lovers* of course.'

Gillan made a sound of disgust in the back of her throat. 'Have lots of them, do you?'

'My family—and by that I mean aunts, uncles et cetera—*think* so. They seem to think that all my trips abroad are because of ladies—something I've never bothered to deny—and they are really quite paranoid that I will marry, have children, and leave my money away from them.'

'But you're young!' she exclaimed. 'They surely can't think you will remain a bachelor just so that you can leave your wealth to your family?'

'No-o,' he denied consideringly, as though he was trying to be absolutely fair, 'but they think I should marry someone known to them. Someone they can—manipulate.'

'Which is why you wanted the fiction of our engagement to remain?'

'Yes.'

'And so you didn't tell me Fran had gone in case I, too, went.'

He nodded.

'And that was why you kissed me the second time? Because you saw someone above us—someone you knew, one of the cousins? Someone who needed to be convinced that we *were* lover-like?'

'A *friend* of a cousin. The clans are gathering,' he explained with a small smile. 'One by one they will come to look you over.'

'And so you needed to know, idly, of course,' she added tartly, 'whether I was capable of acting the lover, whether I had any experience to call on.'

'Something like that. It was just a thought.'

'And, having thought it, having allowed Julia to think it, it didn't occur to you that I might actually mind?'

'No.'

'No? *No?* What do you mean, no?' she demanded, scandalised. 'You think I lend my body to anyone who asks?'

He gave an astonished grunt of amusement and shook his head. 'No, Gillan, I didn't think that.'

'Then what did you think?'

He hesitated, stared at her, and slowly shook his head. 'I never plant suggestions,' he said softly.

'And what is that supposed to mean?'

'It means, Miss Hart, that I might have been wrong.'

'About what?'

He shook his head again.

Slamming her cup down, she stated angrily, 'You really are the most autocratic, aggravating man I've ever met! I've had days like I've never had before! I've been insulted, propositioned, accused...engaged! Whipped off in helicopters, told to be a chaperon... I don't *have* days like this! My life is *ordinary*, well planned! And stop smiling, damn you!'

He comically straightened his face.

Gillan wasn't in the least amused. 'And is this army of wannabees likely to come and try to get rid of me?'

He didn't answer, which she took as an affirmative.

'And what form will this getting-rid-of-me take? Violence?' she asked with pithy interest.

'This is Gozo,' he said drily, 'not Sicily.' Searching her face, he asked quietly, 'Why *did* you come? The real reason, Gillan.'

'I've already told you! For a holiday! And I really cannot comprehend why I'm not upstairs packing my bags and storming out! I *should* be!'

'Yes,' he agreed absently as he continued to watch her. 'You didn't come for me?'

'I beg your pardon?' she asked icily.

He gave a small smile. 'My problem is, I don't know how much I can trust you.'

'Trust me for *what*?' she demanded in exasperation.

Still staring at her, his expression thoughtful, he finally murmured, 'When you first came—no, when I knew you were coming, I assumed Nerina had invited you for me.'

'As a photographer.' She nodded. 'But you said—'

'No. *For* me.'

'*For* you?' she demanded in bewilderment. 'What do you mean, *for* you?'

'Oh, lover, mistress, friend,' he said casually.

'*Lov*...? Are you *mad*?'

'No.'

Disbelieving, boneless, she slumped back at the table, stared blindly at the man before her. 'She invited me...told you...? No, I can't *believe* she would do that,' she continued disjointedly. 'I mean, *why*? How could she possibly think...? You must have misunderstood.'

'No, no misunderstanding.'

'She *told* you?'

He nodded.

'That she had invited me *for you*? To be a...?'

He nodded, watched, waited.

'Don't keep nodding!' she ordered almost hysterically. 'And *that's* why...'

'Your command of the language is slipping again,' he reproved her softly.

'What?' she asked blankly. Still on her own treadmill, she repeated incredulously, 'How could she *do* that? And *why*?'

'She likes you,' he said simply.

'*Likes* me? *Likes* me? And liking me will make you... I mean, how could she suppose...?'

'Mmm,' he agreed in some amusement as he watched her struggling for clarity.

'And you thought...?'

'Mmm-hmm.'

Flinging up her head, seeing his amusement, she snapped crossly. 'And *that's* why you kissed me so brutally the first time, why you thought I was angling for it. You thought that was why I'd taken the boat out.'

'Yes.'

'My God!' she exploded furiously. 'Your conceit is enormous!'

Unbelievably, he laughed, gave a little inclination of his head. 'Yes,' he agreed, 'my conceit is enormous—in direct proportion to my wealth. There aren't that many of us, you see. Not enough millionaires to go around.'

'So, seeing as you thought that was why I'd come, you decided to use me for your own ends.'

'Mmm. And then I learned of our engagement...'

'That's ruthless.'

'Life is ruthless. Grow up, Miss Hart.'

'Don't start that again,' she muttered furiously.

'But you assured me,' he murmured blandly, 'that only friends use Christian names. And I'm not entirely sure we could be called *friends*.'

'I'm damned sure we couldn't be called friends! But that's why she went off to Sicily, isn't it? Because she'd told everyone we were engaged and was frightened of facing us—me.'

'I imagine so.'

'But, even without the engagement, she'd already invited me for you,' she murmured disbelievingly. 'Did she really think I'd be able to seduce you?' she demanded incredulously. 'That *I* would?'

'Oh, I'm sure you do yourself an injustice, Miss Hart,' he mocked smoothly. 'There's probably any number of men you could seduce.'

Staring at him, eyes narrowed, she gave a sweet smile. 'Why, thank you, Mr Micallef; you relieve my mind greatly. Perhaps you'd care to point them out!'

His lips twitched.

Warming to her theme, she demanded, 'And does your sister know you so little that she thought you'd be *willing* to be seduced?'

With a quirky smile, he shook his head.

'She thought I might *grow* on you?'

'She obviously has a high regard for your powers of persuasion,' he agreed admiringly.

'She must have! I don't think I've ever heard anything so shatter-brained in my life!'

'She's a romantic,' he explained, as though that made everything crystal-clear. 'Reads a lot of novels.'

'She also sounds as though she needs a psychiatrist! No wonder you were so poky.'

'Poky? Oh, surely not. Smooth, perhaps—urbane. But poky? Never.'

Giving him a look of disgust, she asked nicely, 'And how *could* she have overlooked the fact that you like your women with long hair?'

'An oversight,' he agreed. 'Perhaps she hoped the hot weather would make it grow quickly. She didn't ask you to wear a wig?'

'No,' she denied stonily. 'And I don't find this amusing! But it would have served you right if you'd fallen wildly in love with me and I'd been totally immune to your charms and rebuffed you, wouldn't it?'

'And that's a scenario that fills you with glee, is it? But you aren't immune, are you?' he asked softly.

Staring at him in disbelief that he could say anything so—ungentlemanly, her cheeks flushed scarlet, she shoved herself to her feet and walked out.

'Miss Hart?' he called silkily.

She halted, kept her back to him.

'*Didn't* you know?'

'No,' she denied flatly.

'Then I apologise.'

'*Apologise?*' She swung round. Stalking back into the room, she stormed, 'I don't *want* your apology. What I *want* is to go home, to sanity!'

There was a token tap on the front door, then the sound of it opening, and a soft, feminine voice calling, 'Refalo?'

A ruthlessly attractive smile stretched his mouth, and his eyes widened to reveal a gleam of unholy amusement. With two swift steps, he reached her.

'Don't you dare,' she warned throatily.

'Dare?' he mocked. 'Didn't you know you should never dare entrepreneurs? It's their meat and drink, my dear Miss Hart.'

The click of high heels along the hall coincided with his kiss.

Her hands bunched on his shoulders, she tried to shove him away.

He smiled. Like a shark. Refused to be shoved. Turning his head, hands roving seductively up and down her back, causing all sorts of damage to her nervous system, he surveyed the young woman hovering in the doorway wearing a designer dress and a confident smile.

'Diana,' he greeted her drily. 'In the area, were you? Just passing by?'

The smile vanished. 'You can be so *rude*.' She pouted.

Unmoved by the face, figure or pout, he drawled, 'I get lots of practice. Don't slam the door on your way out.'

'You don't mean that.'

'Don't I?'

With uncertainty in her dark brown eyes, then certainty, she glared at him, gave Gillan a comprehensive glance of distaste, and walked out. The front door was slammed.

'One,' he counted softly as he returned his gaze to Gillan.

'One what?' she demanded stormily.

'One of the many. Diana is one of the friends of a cousin I mentioned earlier.'

'And she was the one who was standing above us when you...?'

'Mmm,' he agreed helpfully. 'And you really must learn not to flinch every time I touch you.'

'Then don't touch me!'

He grinned. 'You don't mean that. Are you sure you wouldn't like to stay? It could be fun.'

With her breathing restricted because his warm hands were still causing such havoc, she took a deep breath and stepped back. 'For whom?' she asked stonily.

'It might even cure you of your infatuation.'

'I don't have an infatuation! What I have is a disturbing inability to see past the impact of your eyes!'

'Devastating impact,' he corrected her humorously. 'Shall I wear dark glasses?'

'No,' she said flatly. Turning on her heel, she stalked out with as much dignity as she could muster and went upstairs to her room.

Lying in bed, furious with him, with herself, with Nerina, wishing so badly that she had handled everything differently, she sighed. She should have been amused, quirky, laughing at her obsession with his eyes.

And how could Nerina have *done* such a thing, put her in such an impossible position? How, for one moment, could she have thought that ordinary Gillan Hart could have attracted her brother? Didn't she *see* him as other women saw him? Apparently not.

And behind all her soul-searchings, her musings was the memory of sea water dripping down a naked chest— a very tanned naked chest—of a kiss that had seared. And her tongue traced again that slight puffiness of her inner lip.

With a groan, she turned over, buried her face in the pillow. Just thinking about it aroused her. What would it be like to have him in bed beside her, naked, warm, loving? Clenching her eyes tight, she turned her head the other way, idly smoothed the other pillow, imagined it was... Jerking upright, throwing off the thin coverlet, she hunched herself against the headboard, knees drawn up to her chest. This was *absurd*. And she was hot. How could people sleep in this heat?

Getting up, she turned on the overhead fan and padded into the bathroom. Stripping off her damp nightie, she stood under the shower, and she didn't even care if he heard the water running. Didn't care if he was amused.

But why had it been *urgent* that she come? she wondered with a small frown. Inviting her for her brother's amusement was one thing, but why had it been urgent? Nerina had definitely emphasised the urgency of her visit. Why?

She eventually slept, and woke up feeling heavy-eyed, but with the determination not to be routed any more. Wearing shorts and a loose top—and she didn't care what anyone said; she had nice *legs*—she walked into the dining room and found Refalo there. He was wearing dark wraparound sunglasses.

She stared at him, remembered all the things he had said, done, felt that wretched curl in her stomach, thought of the humiliation, but it still didn't stop her lips from twitching. Biting them hard, she fought to contain a snort, and couldn't.

'Better?' he asked softly.

'No.' And it wasn't. Not being able to see his eyes at all was very disconcerting. 'I don't even know why I'm bothering to talk to you. You've insulted me—'

'Kissed you.'

'Stop it,' she warned. 'Just stop right there.'

He smiled, pushed the basket of rolls nearer to her, and even poured her coffee.

'Can we start again? From the beginning? In mitigation, there were, actually, quite a lot of reasons for my mistrust. Please?'

'Why?' she asked suspiciously. 'Because you want the engagement to continue?'

'Partly,' he agreed honestly. 'And partly because I've been enjoying our sparring. I think I might even like you.'

'Oh, wow.'

He laughed—an infectious little chuckle that really rather eroded her defences.

'Tell me about you,' he ordered mildly.

'You know about me; you had me investigated, remember?' She reached for a roll and slowly buttered it.

'So I did. You like travelling?'

Eyeing him for a moment in silence, she gave in. Talking might at least disperse her feelings. 'I suppose.' She shrugged. 'I don't *mind* it, if that's what you're asking. I go where the work takes me, and I'm grateful to have it.'

'You don't want to marry, have children?'

With a wry smile, she murmured, 'Despite your opinion to the contrary, it doesn't fill my every waking thought. But if it happens, it happens.'

'An independent lady.'

'Mmm.' Slanting him an amused glance, and, however hard it was, she was determined to be amused—she said, 'I'm nearly thirty; I had one disastrous relationship in my early twenties, since then I have neither tumbled into love nor become inflamed with unbridled passion, and perhaps more to the point, no man has professed such a desire for me. Perhaps no one ever will, in which case—'

'You will lead a celibate life?'

A little twinkle in her eyes, she asked softly, 'Will I?'

He laughed. 'A liberated lady?'

'A lady who makes the most of what she has.'

'Perhaps that's why Nerina nominated you for the post of...'

'Courtesan?' she asked softly, and he smiled again.

'Wife is what I think she had in mind,' he said drily.

'She can't really be that naïve.'

'Yes,' he said, without apparent thought for whether he might hurt her or not, 'she can.'

And that told you, Gillan Hart. But you are *amused*, remember? 'Don't *you* want to get married?'

'I don't know,' he said thoughtfully. Finishing his coffee, he placed his cup tidily in the saucer and returned it to the tray. 'Certainly not to anyone I have so far met.'

'And yet you must have... You can't be...'

He grinned. 'Celibate? Gay?'

'Neither, I would guess.'

He gave a mocking little inclination of his head.

'But?' she prompted. There had to be a but. 'Tell me,' she persuaded softly. 'I am, as they say, utterly fascinated.'

And attracted, and off balance, and I want to be kissed again, just for pleasure. She would probably even allow him to persuade her to be his pretend lover, because she had thought about that rather a lot during the night. Perhaps she was going mad. How could she even contemplate something so absurd? How could she be having wry conversations with a man she wanted to strip naked and—ravage? But she was doing fine, she praised herself—despite that inner yearning, her fascination with him. He was an amusing companion, when lust was held at bay.

'Why are you smiling?'

'Wicked thoughts. Go on.'

He chuckled. 'I think I'd rather hear about the wicked thoughts.'

'You like your women with long hair. Go *on*!'

'I don't know that there's anything to go on with. Except disillusionment with the fair sex. I told you about being propositioned by designing women?'

She nodded.

'I like to be free. You said you were surprised that you were able to find me so easily, that you expected millionaires to be more hedged about with security. I don't know how it is in England, or the States, but here everyone knows me, and it would be absurd to hide, put security grilles round my houses, have a bodyguard, be driven everywhere.

'Apart from Nerina, who knows never to put herself in a dangerous situation, I have no immediate family that could be kidnapped, held to ransom. Anyway, it's absurd,' he said impatiently. 'Most of my money is tied up in the corporation; the assets wouldn't be readily realised. And I would *hate* to live like that—not to be free to do as I wanted, when I wanted. What is the point of having money if you aren't free to spend it? No, the only problem I have is women wanting to *help* me spend it.'

Nodding sagely, she stated, 'Tight. I guessed it. Knew there had to be a flaw in the perfection.'

Lips pursed humorously, he stared at her—well, she assumed he was staring at her; certainly the dark glasses were turned in her direction.

'Which brings us back to us. And so, do we know,' she continued blithely, 'what current story is going round?'

'Mmm.'

Leaning forward with an air of confidentiality, she whispered, 'Do tell. We're still engaged?'

'Possibly.' Ticking off the various rumours on his fingers, he began, 'You either, one, came out ahead of Francesca to prepare the ground—an opportunity too good to miss—'

'I'm in *cahoots* with Francesca?'

'Mmm. Don't interrupt. Or, two, you are a lady of— um—easy virtue whom I met on my travels and I have handsomely paid you to pretend an engagement. Three, you are my current mistress, with the same conditions. And four, for some reason one or two have hinted at a secret wedding too.'

'A *secret* wedding?'

'Mmm.'

'But Julia and Diana have seen me,' she stated understandingly, 'Seen my lack of glamour. So they don't believe that one, do they?'

'No-o,' he agreed. 'Although why your lack of glamour should have anything to do with it, I don't know.'

'Yes, you do,' she argued. 'Julia and Diana are both glamorous and sophisticated, and women like that would judge me by my ordinariness, my casual clothes. Not even *expensive* casual clothes. They would look at me and find it inconceivable that you would want someone like me.'

'Would they?'

'Yes. Believe me, Refalo, I *know* what women like that think.'

'Do you?' He gave a small smile and added provocatively, 'But they're still worried. They apparently thought you looked determined.'

'Ah.' She grinned. 'Might I be of a jealous disposition?'

He laughed, nodded. 'Fiercely possessive.'

'And which rumour do you favour?' she asked interestedly. 'The lady of ill repute?'

'Certainly not. I favour the secret wedding.'

Somewhat surprised, she exclaimed, 'But why?'

'Because a wife would be more difficult for them to get rid of than a mistress.'

'Ah, yes, but when you *did* want to get rid of me... Messy divorce,' she mused. 'Half your fortune wiped away at one stroke... I mean, if I'm *determined*, I'd want compensation, wouldn't I? You haven't thought this through properly.'

'Obviously not,' he agreed, with a narrow stare she didn't see.

'But what I would *like* to know,' she continued, 'is how long you thought you'd be able to keep me in the dark about Fran not being here. How long before you were caught rumpling her bed as though she'd been using it? I assume it *was* you?'

'Mmm. Turning on her shower, leaving things lying around...'

'Seems a bit excessive, doesn't it?'

'I was a man driven. Still driven.'

'And how many women—just a rough estimate will be sufficient—are likely to come checking out the opposition? Two? Four? A lot? And don't look at me like a little boy who's been caught raiding the cookie jar. How many?'

'How do you know I'm looking at you like anything? You can't see my eyes.' With another smile, he pushed the stack of envelopes that had been by his plate towards her. 'Julia,' he informed her softly, 'has been busy.'

Glancing down, then back to his face, she asked, 'What are they?'

'Invitations to family gatherings.'

'For both of us?'

'Mmm.'

'To look me over?'

'Mmm.'

She gave a delightfully roguish grin. 'Going to buy me a posh frock?'

He shook his head.

Nodding sagely, she murmured, 'That's right; look after the pennies and the pounds will look after themselves. And Julia?'

'Julia?'

'Mmm. Is she one of the women desirous of sharing your wealth?'

'No-o, Julia is happily married—but she has a very good friend...' Leaving the sentence hanging, he waited.

'And you didn't expect me to *mind* about Nerina's little plot? Once you'd discovered I wasn't in cahoots with her, of course.'

'Of course,' he agreed smoothly. 'And yes, I expected you to be furious. As you were. I also expected you to pack your bags and flounce off.'

'I'm not a flouncer. I don't have the equipment for it. And then what?'

'I would have said you'd had to leave, that you had only come for a short visit and that I would be seeing you later in England.'

'You would have let me go without a qualm because I wasn't important, wasn't known, and you couldn't have cared less about my feelings in all this.'

'Which makes me the most arrogant, ruthless, selfish...?' he began queryingly.

'Those accusations have obviously been levelled before.'

'Oh, yes, with a frequency that makes them boring.'

'Hmm. And now?'

'Ah, now.'

Moving her eyes away, her amused façade slipping slightly, she asked quietly, 'Do you manipulate everyone?'

'Of course.'

'Including Nerina?'

'Especially Nerina. How are the photographs coming along?'

'Nearly finished. Today should do it. If you could get them developed...?'

He nodded, continued to watch her. 'Nerina would be pleased if...' he began thoughtfully.

'Nerina would *not* be pleased. Nerina would be hurt when she found out that we'd been less than honest.' Then she winced as she remembered that *she* was being less than honest—but she couldn't tell him because she had no right.

'It would help me out,' he murmured.

Snatching her attention back to him, burying the hurt deep inside, she demanded humorously, 'Now why would I want to help you out?' She finished her roll and reached for another one. She broke it in half and carefully spread it with butter and apricot preserve. 'Hmm?' she queried with a tiny smile.

'I'll take my glasses off,' he threatened.

'Go *away*,' she laughed.

Glancing at his watch, he nodded. 'I have to collect the *Christina* from Sliema—Valletta,' he substituted, in case she didn't know where Sliema was.

'The *Christina*?'

'A yacht.'

'Yours?'

'Yes. Want to come?' he invited casually.

Want to? Oh, yes, she wanted to, couldn't think of anything she'd like better. But alone with him? Watching him work sails, stripped to the waist, maybe... No, that would be foolish. She was coping now, but it was a very fragile composure. She shook her head. 'I have photographs to take, remember?'

He nodded.

'You might *try* to look disappointed,' she reproved him. 'I do have *some* ego.'

He laughed, got to his feet. 'I'll see you later. I should be back late this afternoon.'

'I might not be here,' she murmured.

He merely smiled.

'I mean, I might have finished the photographs and gone home.'

'You might,' he agreed. 'But, being a professional, you would surely want my approval of them first?'

She threw her napkin at him. 'And what are you intending to do about the invitations?'

'Ignore them.'

With a look of disgust, she watched him walk out—then remembered something else. 'Hey!' she called after him, and when he put his head back through the door she asked, 'I thought you were going to see Fran's mother?'

He looked surprised. 'I've already seen her. Yesterday. I got back in time to find you missing, which was why the helicopter was so readily available.' With a vague lift of his hand, he disappeared.

'Refalo!' Shoving back her chair, she chased after him. 'What did she say?'

He sighed, glanced at his watch again, pursed his lips in thought. 'Walk with me; I'll tell you on the way.'

Nodding, automatically snatching up her camera, she fell into step beside him.

'I liked Tom,' he began conversationally.

'Stop being aggravating. What did she say?'

'Very little. Her pregnancy hasn't been easy; she feels ill most of the time. Tom looked long-suffering.'

'And?'

'And he was furious when he found out that Elaine—Fran's mother—wanted recompense.' Glancing down at her, he continued, 'He loves Fran—couldn't love her more if she was his own daughter. He doesn't *understand* her,' he added humorously, 'but he does love her. And he wants her home. I persuaded him to let her stay for a few days.'

'So it *was* innocent?'

'From Franesca's and Tom's point of view, yes. I'm not so certain about Elaine.'

'But you won't pay compensation, will you?'

'No, Miss Hart, I won't pay any compensation.' Halting at the top of the steps, he braced his arms on the railings, stared down at the motor launch tied up at the foot of the steps and waved an acknowledgement to the man standing in the prow. Flicking her a glance, he asked, 'Want to change your mind?'

She shook her head.

He smiled, caught her against him with his free arm, stared down into her startled face, and kissed her. Thoroughly. And with what appeared to be a great deal of satisfaction.

CHAPTER SIX

MOUTH tingling, the warmth of Refalo's arm still apparent, Gillan glanced warily round, saw no one who looked even remotely interested—certainly not any young women who looked desirous of getting rid of her—and dazedly returned her attention to the motor launch that was just moving off. A hand was raised in farewell, and she automatically waved back. With a funny little shudder, she walked back to the villa.

With very little prompting, she could probably fall in love with him. And what would that get her? Heartache—that was what. A dangerous game, she told herself—if she allowed it to continue. Which, of course, she wouldn't. But despite herself, despite her intentions, she liked him—and she certainly liked being touched by him. Was beginning to dwell on it.

Impatient with herself, trying to shove him from her mind, she collected the car keys and went off to finish her photography. Where she couldn't drive, she walked, her mind on Refalo.

Her first impressions—dusty and primitive, hot—were being tempered by the warmth and friendliness of the people, the smiles and good wishes, the mesmerising blue of sea and sky. I'm being seduced, she thought, and the longer I stay, the greater the spell.

She didn't in the least understand why Refalo was flirting with her, because that was what it was. After indifferent detachment, and anger when she'd been out in the boat, he was now being charming, friendly, flirtatious. And not because of his numerous relatives; she didn't buy that story for a moment. If Refalo wanted them off his back, he was quite capable of ruthlessly ordering them away.

So why? It certainly wasn't for her charms. Oh, she was nice enough, attractive enough, she supposed, but hardly the sort of woman to attract a man like Refalo Micallef. But you'd like him to be attracted, wouldn't you, Gillan? said the voice inside her head. Yes, she was honest enough to admit that. But it wouldn't happen, she told herself, so let's be sensible here, hmm?

She had lunch out—sitting outside a small café in a place she didn't know the name of, watching people about their business with an absent gaze. Was he back yet, this man who was turning her world upside down? Even the thought of him quickened her breathing, brought that ache of excitement inside.

The waiter hovering to replenish her coffee cup brought her back to awareness, and she smiled up at him and shook her head. Paying her bill, she hooked her camera bag over her shoulder and walked slowly back to the car.

Driving home—home? How odd to think of it like that—she continued to think about him. Part of her— no, most of her wanted to give in to his blandishments, and the other part—the small, sensible part—said no. No, no, no, no, no. Anyway, he'd probably only been joking, teasing. Yes, that was all it had been.

Finding the villa empty, she went up to her room to shower and change into soft white trousers and a navy and white halter top. Very nautical, she mocked herself.

Returning downstairs, she made herself a cold drink, then found herself walking towards the inlet. *Not* to see if a yacht was moored in the bay, she assured herself; merely to benefit from the sea breeze. Her cold drink still clutched in her hand, she looked down, and felt a stab of disappointment. No yacht.

Barely aware of what she was doing, she descended to the tree-shaded promenade. Perching on a bench, she gazed out to sea, then gave a faint wry smile as she saw a beautiful white yacht round the headland and turn into the bay. There were others lining the railing, also watching the yacht—tourists who commented, pointed, sighed in pleasure and perhaps envy as the sail was lowered, the anchor dropped.

'Miss Hart?'

Startled, she turned, stared up into the weather-beaten face of the boatman who'd hired her the outboard what felt like a lifetime ago. Cesare, she remembered. He grinned, removed the drink from her hand, placed it carefully on the bench and beckoned.

Bewildered, she followed him down the remaining steps, obediently stepped into the small boat moored at the bottom, and without argument, explanation, allowed herself to be rowed out to the *Christina*. A ladder was flung over the side and she automatically climbed up to the deck.

'Hi,' Refalo greeted her. He was still sporting his dark glasses.

'Hi,' she murmured weakly.

'Welcome aboard.'

'Thank you.'

He peered over the rail, waved at Cesare, then gently took her arm. 'Come and inspect my pride and joy.'

He took her forward, showed her gadgets, navigation aids, and Gillan nodded, smiled, like a mechanical doll. He led her aft, opened the door to the cabin and invited her inside. It was dim down there, intimate, cool, and she hesitated until a little prod in her back took away her indecision. Stumbling down, she whirled to face him as he descended. Stood like a fool.

'I don't know what I'm doing here,' she said stupidly.

'Don't you?' he asked softly.

'No. If I hadn't been on the promenade...'

He gave a slow, devastating smile. 'But I knew you would be.'

'No, you didn't.' Her breathing agitated, she felt that squirmy feeling in her stomach, that shock and awareness as he removed his glasses and tossed them onto the nearby bench. She didn't even have the sense to move when he closed the very short distance between them.

'No,' she whispered thickly.

'Yes.' Sliding his fingers into the short hair behind her ears, he stared deep into her eyes, then moved his gaze to her mouth. 'You're quivering,' he murmured softly, seductively.

She made a sound that could have meant anything, clenched her hands tight at her sides. 'There isn't anyone to see us.'

'No.'

'Then why are you doing it—this?'

He gave an odd smile. 'Because it's absurd.'

'What is?'

'This—wanting you.'

Her heart threatening to damage itself irrevocably against her ribcage, her eyes wide, she stared at him like a mesmerised rabbit. She couldn't even *think*.

His mouth parted, drew nearer, and she dragged in a shallow breath, let it out on a shudder as his mouth finally touched hers. With a little jerk, she held still, felt as though she was physically holding herself together as his mouth slowly explored hers. His fingers against her scalp were massaging, soothing, the little fingers playing an erotic tattoo against her nape, until it was too much, too exhausting to remain rigid.

With a little groan, she let all her muscles go at once, slumped against him, grasped his waist for support and shuddered like someone in the grip of fever.

He made a small murmur that sounded like satisfaction and continued to kiss her. His mouth was relentless, and so thorough—so mind-blowingly thorough. Experienced, her mind whispered as she gave in to pleasure and pain, excitement and pure delight.

His strong hands still against her head, gentle, without pressure, his body still, unmoving, he seduced with mouth alone, woke ripples of desire, aroused without effort, until she wanted more, and more and more. Wanted him closer, tighter—wanted all he had to give. Wanted to give all that she had.

She didn't remember leaning into him, didn't remember sliding her hands up his back beneath his shirt; all she was conscious of was his mouth on hers, of a kiss that deepened imperceptibly, of warm skin beneath her fingers, of a heart that felt as though it was trying to break free.

How long could one kiss go on for? she wondered dizzily as she responded to the small shifting movements he made with his mouth. How long? How long? He nibbled at her lips with his strong teeth, nibbled her tongue, and her mouth parted beneath his, her neck arched, her head too heavy, breathing ragged.

Hands still in her hair, he used his elbows to hold her close, touched his thighs intimately against hers, until she felt torn apart inside, a quivering jelly of a girl, mastered, manipulated, incapable of independent thought. And *still* his mouth played with hers, until one hand slid slowly from nape to lower spine, exerted gentle but persistent pressure. She felt his heart jerk, as did hers, his breath arrest, as did hers. They stilled together, drew back their upper bodies and stared into each other's eyes.

Their breathing slowly resumed as they continued to stare at each other. Gillan had no idea what to say or do next. He was the master. In complete control. The next move *had* to be up to him. The next word, the next thought. And he did nothing. Just continued to stare at her. And that in itself was the most arousing thing that had ever happened to her. Lower bodies touching, upper apart, eyes locked in silence. Eternities passed. Aeons. And then he blinked, gave the wryest of wry smiles, hugged her to him, and laughed.

Disbelieving, bewildered, so very aroused, she rested her head on his shoulder and gave a long, shaky sigh.

'We could make this real,' he murmured softly, and it took her a moment to comprehend, hear what he'd said.

'Make what real?' Eyes wide, worried, she queried in panic, 'Have an affair, you mean?'

'Mmm. We get on.'

'We do *not* get on!'

'You fit well in my arms,' he continued, as though she hadn't spoken.

'No,' she denied helplessly as she tried to thrust herself away.

'Keep still,' he ordered softly as he easily held her in place. 'It feels good.'

Oh, God.

'You're nearly thirty...'

'Don't keep saying that!' she wailed. 'I feel...'

'Like a broken bird?' he asked gently.

'Yes. No.' Her breathing all shot to pieces, she searched his face, found nothing to help. 'You said it was absurd,' she croaked.

'Mmm.'

'Well, then. And why is it absurd? I'm not an *antidote*!'

His eyes crinkled. 'No. I meant, absurd that kissing you aroused me.'

Lungs distorted, she just stared at him. 'When?'

'On the promenade, after you "slipped".'

'You weren't aroused. You were angry.'

'Yes, with myself, and at the absurdity of it. Nerina likes you.'

'Nerina got us into this mess! And you can't have an affair with someone just because your sister likes her! You don't even *know* me! Three days ago you didn't even *like* me!'

'Is it really only three days? It feels longer.'

'Well, it isn't!'

'You're attracted to me,' he tried to persuade her wickedly.

'I *know* I am!'

His eyes crinkled. 'It could be good.'

'It could be disastrous! And don't arrogantly assume that just because I'm attracted to you you only have to whistle and I'll come! I have a mind of my own, Refalo, and I'm very strong-willed.'

'I know.' He grinned.

With a humph of despair, trying to ignore the spiralling waves of warmth that were emanating from their touching bodies, she added heatedly, 'You could break my heart!'

'Or you could break mine.'

'Doubtful,' she muttered raggedly.

'You don't think I have a heart?'

'I don't know! Oh, this is crazy!'

'And isn't it allowed to be crazy?' he asked softly.

'Not with *me*, it isn't! People don't behave like this with me! I'm *sensible*!'

He laughed, hugged her briefly, then slowly released her.

Dragging in a deep breath of relief, she stepped back, eyed him warily.

With a faint smile, he leaned back against the door-frame behind him, blocking her escape. 'Didn't you ever wonder how I knew you at the airport?'

'What?' she asked blankly. 'You knew who I was?'

'Mmm.'

'How?'

'I did my own investigating,' he explained easily, and her heart gave a little jerk of worry. 'Talked to people you worked with. I was assured you were professional, well liked, reliable. I watched you work, watched you laugh, persuade people, and I—wondered about you.'

'You were angry with me,' she corrected drily, 'for taking your sister to drug-crazed parties.'

'Mmm,' he agreed humorously. 'But I assumed, then, that it was a casual friendship. I certainly did not expect Nerina to invite you out to Malta.'

'And were less than pleased when she did so,' she stated flatly, relieved that he had made no mention of the trust and her supposed work there. And now that they weren't touching it was easier to be rational.

'Mmm. I don't like being manipulated.'

'Neither do I,' she stated pointedly. 'And *I* didn't manipulate *you*.' Turning away, staring fixedly at the blue curtains across the window, she murmured, 'She treats me like a big sister.'

'I know.'

Giving him an irritated glance, she said, 'Oh, put your glasses back on!'

He laughed, shook his head. 'I won't be able to see what I'm doing.'

Taking another wary step backwards, she demanded, 'And what do you intend to be doing?'

He raised an eyebrow. 'Feeding us, of course.'

'Feeding us?'

'Mmm. I'll rig an awning; we can eat on deck.'

Turning, he ran lightly up the companionway, and moments later she heard sundry thuds and thumps as he, presumably, rigged an awning. Sinking weakly down onto one of the bunks, heart still beating like a trip-hammer, she stared worriedly at nothing.

An affair? she thought almost hysterically. With Refalo Micallef? He must have sunstroke. You didn't have affairs with people you didn't know! Didn't make love for no reason! Except that she'd aroused him that time. He'd said so, hadn't he? She also aroused him now—then...

'Come on; up you come.'

With a little start, a worried little shake of her head, she climbed up to the deck and gave a small smile at the sight of a table and two cushioned chairs set under a striped awning. She sat down.

Moments later, he brought her up a glass of chilled white wine.

'Thank you,' she murmured helplessly.

'My pleasure. Don't drink the local red,' he warned smilingly. 'Ever. It's full of chemicals. It will make you ill. And we don't want you ill, do we? Will you excuse me? I have to see to the meal.'

'Complicated, is it?'

A small dimple appeared in his cheek.

With another little shake of her head, she asked idly, 'Am I in view of anyone important?'

'Why?'

'I thought I might wave.'

He laughed, patted her shoulder in a kindly fashion and disappeared below. Sipping her wine, idly watching the tourists on the promenade who were watching her, she waved anyway. They waved back. With a little chuckle, she allowed her tense muscles to relax. Go with the flow, Gillan. Go with the flow. He was joking. The man had a very odd sense of humour.

As he bustled back and forth to lay the table, put out fresh bread rolls, salad, she watched him with a bemused expression, continued to drink her wine, then gave a little gurgle of infectious laughter. If only her friends could see her now. They wouldn't believe it. *She* didn't believe it! A devastating millionaire, a fancy yacht...

Still smiling, she tilted back her head, stared up at the rigging, listened to the soft sounds the wind made as it passed through it, and sighed. 'Isn't it allowed to be crazy?' he'd asked. Why not? She could be dead tomorrow. Hastily touching her fingers to the wooden deck, just in case she'd alerted some vengeful god, she gave a wry smile at her superstition—but one never knew...

'Why the smile?' Refalo queried as he returned, carrying two large plates piled high with seafood. Placing one before her, he put his opposite, sat down, then leapt up again. 'Forgot something.'

Hurrying away, he returned seconds later and tossed a large manila envelope onto her lap. 'Photographs.'

'Mine?'

'Of course, yours.'

'*And?*' she queried.

'You tell me.'

With an exasperated grunt, she opened the envelope and spilled the enlargements onto the table beside her plate. The top ones were those she'd taken from the helicopter. 'Not bad—not bad at all,' she murmured

thoughtfully as she slowly examined them, but her mind
was only half on the photographs. The other half was
on the man sitting opposite her.

Still feeling incredibly jerky and unsettled, she forced
herself to concentrate on the snaps. Always critical of
herself, lips pursed, she sifted through them, automatically set aside those she didn't like, then separated those
for the brochure from those of the damaged vessel.

'Eat your meal,' Refalo ordered softly.

Absently picking up her fork, she took a mouthful,
her attention still fixed on the photographs. Staring at
those she'd taken of Calypso's Cave, she muttered in
irritation, 'I *knew* those wouldn't work.'

'Tell me why,' he said quietly.

'Too impatient. The light was wrong; I was hot...
Have you ever climbed up there?' she demanded, looking
up, then quickly looking away again, felt warmth suf-
fuse her.

'Mmm.'

'Yes, well, I'll have to do those again. But the
others...' Lips still pursed, she leaned back to consider
them. 'Good detail on the temple...'

'Eat your meal,' he repeated.

With a nod, she put them down and began to eat, her
mind still on Refalo, still on the photographs, what she
could do to improve those she didn't like. Maybe another
angle... Certainly a different time of day. Early morning,
perhaps... 'Which way does the cave face?'

'North.'

She nodded. 'Early morning, then.' Glancing at him,
seeing the faint smile on his mouth, she raised a querying eyebrow. 'What?' she asked defensively.

He shook his head, topped up their glasses from the
wine bottle resting in the ice bucket, and continued with
his own meal.

Still staring at him, she demanded, 'Aren't you going to tell me what you think of them?'

'You know what I think of them.'

'No, I don't. How would I know?'

'Because you're a professional and far more critical than I would ever be. If you think them good...'

'I think *some* of them are good.'

'Good enough for my brochure?'

'Yes.'

'Then I agree.' Eyeing her somewhat mockingly, he asked, 'Were you expecting praise?'

'No.'

'Liar.'

'It's nice to be *appreciated*!'

'They are appreciated, and I didn't labour over a hot stove for the meal to be ignored. Eat! And take that miffy look off your face.'

Flicking him a glance, mouth scrunched up, she suddenly smiled. 'OK. *I* think you were lucky to get me.'

'So do I,' he said softly, and she somehow didn't think he meant as a photographer. Cheeks pink, alarm altering her breathing, she concentrated on her meal.

'I thought the others were quite good,' he commented blandly.

'Mmm. For a beginner.'

He laughed.

Shelling the last prawn and popping it into her mouth, she gave him a wary smile. 'A truly excellent meal. Thank you.'

He raised his glass in a silent toast. Collecting their plates, he removed them and, as though he had timed it to perfection, just as he placed their coffee before them the sun sank out of sight, leaving them in velvet darkness. The lights from the town and the promenade twinkled

like stars, the soft wind soughed through the rigging—
and Refalo moved his chair next to hers.

'Better view,' he murmured softly as her muscles
tightened in self-defence.

'Of what?' she asked in alarm.

'The lights, of course.'

'Oh.'

Stomach cramping, awareness washing over her in
waves, she stared at her coffee cup, reached out to put
in sugar with a hand that felt alien, unconnected.

He blew softly on her ear, and she shivered.

'Look at me.'

'No,' she said thickly.

Reaching out, he gently turned her face towards him.
Their noses almost touched.

'You have a nice mouth.'

'Yes. No,' she muttered distractedly. 'I mean, thank
you.'

'You're welcome.'

Oh, God. His voice was pure seduction, his stillness
so damnably arousing. 'This isn't fair,' she moaned.

'No.'

'Then why are you doing it?'

'Don't you want me to?' he asked conversationally.

'Yes. No. I can't even *breathe*.'

'Then I'll do it for you.' His voice a soft whisper of
sound, eyes still fixed unwaveringly on hers, he placed
one hand on her midriff and gently applied pressure,
placed one hand on the back of her neck, and applied
a different pressure until their mouths met, softly, tan-
talisingly, and then lingeringly, until Gillan wanted to
throw caution to the winds, hold him impossibly tight,
strip him naked, make love to him urgently, desperately,
completely.

He rose, still holding her, so that she was forced to rise too. He kicked their chairs away and lowered her to the deck, out of sight of land—out of sight of everyone and everything. Rescuing the cushions one-handed, he put them side by side, lowered her head to one, put his own on the other, continued to mesmerise her with his beautiful eyes, and replaced his hand on her midriff.

'I can feel your heart beating,' he murmured, his face so serious, his voice so captivating. 'Feel mine.'

She didn't want to, didn't want this to go any further. So why, then, did she raise her arm? An arm that felt boneless. Why did she place her hand on his chest to feel the warmth of him, the faint beat of his heart? But her hand didn't want to lie quiescent; it wanted to rove, touch, feel, and so it did—smoothed across his broad chest, lingered briefly on his upper arm, moved to his neck, his ear, the hair at his nape—and the sighing breath she took was enormous.

'Refalo...'

'Shh.'

'But—'

'Shh.'

Worried, aching, drowning in diamond-bright eyes, yet soothed by the lapping water against the hull, the gentle rocking on the swell, she moved her fingers to his mouth, traced the outline, watched the pink fingernail as it parted his lips, parted her own in unconscious echo, moved without knowing she did so until her mouth could touch his, her finger trapped between.

Closing her eyes, she savoured the feel of him, the taste, the sheer pleasure of lying like this, touching like this, until desire began to build to impossible levels, until she began to quiver with the effort of holding herself still, until her muscles began to cramp painfully from the tension. Unaware of her soft moans, the voiceless pleas, she moved one leg across his, gasped at the contact, the new heat generated, raised her eyes to his, not knowing of the plea in her own.

'I don't know what I'm doing,' she whispered helplessly. 'Oh, Refalo, what am I *doing*?'

'All the things you've ever wanted to,' he breathed in a voice grown husky. 'You can do them now. To me.'

Shocked, excited, frightened, she shook her head, closed her eyes in defeat, rested her forehead against his. 'I can't.'

Moving her gently back to her cushion, he rolled to cover her, stare down into her eyes. 'No?' he asked gently.

She shook her head.

'Because you don't want to?'

'No,' she said honestly, 'because I *do* want to. But I don't, can't... Is it a game?' she pleaded, praying it wasn't.

'No,' he denied. 'I don't play those sorts of games.'

'Then why? Because of your relations?'

'No, not even because of them.' Rolling back onto his own cushion, ankles crossed, he sought for her hand, then held it warmly in both of his. Staring up at the sky, he continued, 'Not a whim, not a game. Perhaps tiredness, a desire for something—peaceful. Do you know, this is the first time I've really relaxed with a woman since before Nerina was diagnosed as having leukaemia? And it feels—good.

'Everything—all my thoughts, my will, my being— has been focused on my little sister. I ran the business, I talked, laughed, presumably made sense, but it was only a small portion of me that took part in life. And it didn't matter—none of it mattered—only Nerina. All my time was for her. In case,' he added sombrely.

'But now, please God, she's going to be all right; now I can think a little bit about me. Time to breathe, time to—relax.' Turning his head towards hers, he gave a faint smile, squeezed her hand.

'That's why she wanted you for me. She's been anguishing over her big brother not having time for his own life. As if it mattered. She thinks I should be married, with babies, thinks that's what I yearn for, thinks I shouldn't have put my life on hold for her. But I never found anyone I wanted to marry, never thought I wanted children—until Francesca turned up. And then I suddenly thought— It would be nice to be a father.

'And then Julia's misunderstanding fuelled an idea. Part of me was against it, and part of me was aroused by the thought of it. But I still didn't know if I could trust you. Then wanting to kiss you became an—obsession.'

'Obsession?' she whispered worriedly.

'Mmm. You don't flirt with me, throw out lures—it made a refreshing change,' he murmured with a whimsical smile, a teasing sideways glance. 'Any other woman of my acquaintance would have taken my side against Francesca, would have been outraged, insisted I send her home.'

'But you thought I was in cahoots with her.'

'Thought you *might* be. You argue with me, berate me . . .'

'And you aren't used to that, are you?' she asked a little sadly.

'No. Not because I want it that way, expect it that way, but most people either want something from me and are, therefore—'

'Toadying?' she put in tartly.

He grinned, squeezed her hand. 'Or they seem a little afraid of me.'

'I'm not surprised. You talk to people as though *daring* them to argue with you!'

'You dared. It could be fun,' he said softly, persuasively. 'You're independent, nice to be with, intelligent, nice to kiss. You're extraordinarily attractive, and you have a quirky smile.'

'But short hair,' she murmured foolishly.

'Mmm. Incipient middle age, do you think?' he asked with a grin. 'This restlessness?'

'I don't know.' And she didn't.

'Don't you get restless, Gillan?'

'Yes,' she said slowly, and realised it was true. 'But it's not a *specific* restlessness—and I'm certainly not middle-aged!'

He chuckled. Turning towards her, idly stroking one finger down her cheek, he asked softly, 'Want to play? See where it leads?'

Searching his eyes—those beautiful diamond-bright eyes—she exclaimed helplessly, 'I don't know!' People don't behave like this, she kept thinking. People *don't*.

'Do you know how old I am?' he asked quietly, and she shook her head. 'Thirty-seven, and I don't ever remember taking a holiday. I shall take one now.'

'What about your business?'

'Oh, I think it can manage without me for a few days. I have excellent staff, and if I'm needed I'm only a phone call away. We could go sailing, diving...'

'I have to be in Tunisia at the end of next week—a photo shoot.'

'Then why not give it until the end of next week?'

'And all your relatives? Friends of relatives?'

He grinned rather wickedly. 'Can I help what they think? But if they think what I hope they will think then that's all well and good, isn't it?'

'So long as they don't try to bump me off,' she retorted drily.

'They won't. Come on; if you won't let me make love to you, let's go home.'

Home. There was that word again.

Drawing himself up until he was sitting cross-legged, her hand still held in his, he asked gently, 'Why so sad?'

'Sad? Is that how I looked?'

'Mmm.'

With a little shake of her head, she stared up at the rigging at the stars that were just coming out. 'Why did you name her *Christina*?'

'After my mother.'

'That's nice. She died, didn't she?'

'Yes. When Nerina was sixteen. We thought at first that her listlessness, her apathy was due to her mother's death...'

'And, instead of which, it was leukaemia.'

'Yes,' he agreed sombrely. 'You have a mother?'

She shook her head. 'She died a long time ago.'

'Father?'

'No...' A little break shook her voice, and she tried to disguise it with a cough; she waited until she was able to go on. 'He died last year. Sorry,' she whispered huskily. 'It still hurts.' Trying to smile, a sheen of tears in her eyes, she added softly, 'It will be a while yet before I can talk about him. I miss him so much.'

And that was why the word 'home' was so poignant, because she no longer had one. Her flat wasn't home; it didn't hold the echo of childish laughter, smell of baking, have the comforting bulk of her father sitting in his favourite chair.

'It's the hardest thing in the world to lose a father,' he commented quietly. 'Or a child.'

'Yes.' Or a mother.

With a return to briskness, he lifted her hand, lightly kissed her fingers and released it. 'I'll clear up, and then we'll go home.'

Whilst he busied himself with clearing away the awning, table and chairs, locked up the cabin, she sat quietly watching the stars.

With a smile that was gentle, companionable, he reached to pull her upright, tossed the dinghy over the side, climbed down to secure the painter, and waited for her to join him.

'Fortunate I wore trousers.'

'For you, perhaps.' He smiled as he began to row them to the shore.

'Voyeur,' she scolded softly.

They walked in peaceful silence to the villa, their clasped hands swinging between them—and found Fran waiting.

He groaned, too softly for Fran to hear, then greeted her easily, 'Hello.'

'I came back,' she stated with her customary aggression.

'So I see.'

'I didn't like them.'

'No,' he agreed, a small twitch to his lips. 'I don't like them much either.'

'Can I stay?'

'Certainly.'

The look of astonishment on her face was really quite comical. 'I can?'

'Of course.'

'I didn't think you liked me!'

'I don't know you, so how can I know if I like or dislike you?'

'Doesn't stop most people,' she grumbled, and he smiled. Eyeing him almost warily as Gillan had earlier, she blurted out, 'They kept talking about you.'

'Did they?' he asked mildly.

'Yes. Don't you want to know what they said?'

'Not particularly. Have you eaten?'

'Yes.' Staring at him with a great deal of suspicious defiance, she stated baldly, 'You're different.'

'Am I?'

'Yes.' Turning her attention to Gillan, she added, 'They talked about you too.'

'Wicked interloper?' Gillan queried with a smile.

Relaxing fractionally, Fran giggled, looked momentarily young and pleasant, then sobered, looked embarrassed. 'They said...kept asking me if you were—' Breaking off in confusion, she went pink.

'Lovers?' Refalo supplied helpfully as he released Gillan's hand and gently hooked her to stand within the circle of his arm.

'Yes.'

'And what did you say?'

'That I didn't know... That... Well, it isn't anything to do with me, is it?'

'So it isn't,' he agreed, and she gave a funny little grin.

'I mean, *I* don't care what you get up to.' When he didn't answer, merely waited, that small smile on his mouth, she blurted out, 'They even said you might be secretly married!'

'Mmm.'

'And are you?'

'It's a secret,' he said blandly.

A little twitch to her lips, confusion in her eyes, she looked at Gillan. 'Are you?'

She shook her head. 'Don't tell.'

She giggled. 'I won't.'

'Good.'

Clearly still baffled, she asked Refalo, 'But why allow them to *think* you are?'

'Wouldn't you,' he asked humorously, 'with relatives like mine, allow them to think *anything* to keep them off your back?'

'Yeah. I suppose. I'm sorry your sister was ill,' she added quietly.

'Thank you.'

'They talked about her as well.'

'They talk about everyone,' he said repressively, and in clear warning that he wouldn't accept *her* doing any gossiping.

'Can I go to bed?'

He nodded, amused again.

'I won't intrude,' she added stiffly.

'You aren't intruding,' he said gently. Releasing Gillan, dropping a light kiss on her hair in parting, he added, 'Come, I'll even carry your bag up for you.' Removing the carrier bag she held clasped to her chest, he urged her towards the doorway.

'Goodnight,' she called to Gillan over her shoulder.

'Goodnight.'

'I wish you *were* my father!' she heard Fran exclaim as they walked along the hall.

'I almost wish it too,' he answered gently. 'Did you learn anything about Nico?'

'Yeah,' she sighed.

'Yes,' he corrected her. He sounded as though he was smiling.

Walking over to the French windows, Gillan stared out, gave a wry smile. Now who was the chaperon?

* * *

They spent three glorious days sailing, diving, swimming, playing, and Fran lost her sulky air, became instead the happy, uninhibited teenager she was meant to be, had probably been before all the trouble had blown up at home. Refalo was patient with her, kind, amused, and, watching him Gillan found that liking and awareness had probably already edged into something perilously close to love. He kissed her lightly in passing, smiled at her, teased her, sometimes looked at her with a great deal of warmth, but there was no seduction—and she wasn't sure if she was grateful.

She wanted him, wanted to feel his warmth against her, wanted to ease the ache that was building inside. And she wished he wouldn't wear shorts. The sight of his long, tanned legs bothered her. The sight of his naked chest bothered her—the way he swam, like a dolphin, the way he moved. In fact, every single thing about him bothered her.

And on the Sunday Tom telephoned, to say that Francesca had a baby brother.

'Do I have to go home?' she blurted out, looking almost panicky.

'I think so,' Refalo said gently.

'But what will they say?'

'That it's nice to have you back, that they've missed you—and come and look at your baby brother. But first,' he continued, 'we need to buy him a present, don't we?'

'Yes,' she agreed eagerly. 'We could do that, couldn't we?'

'Of course we could. We'll go into Rabat.' Touching his fingers to her hair, he soothed her gently, 'It will be all right.'

'Yes. He didn't say he was cross? Didn't want to shout at me?'

'Why would he? He loves you.'

'But I won't go back to boarding school!'

'Then tell them—tell them why. Don't shut them out, Fran. They did what they thought was best for you.' With a wry smile, he added, 'But adults don't always know what is best for the young.'

'My mother will go spare,' she said gloomily.

'No, she won't. She'll need you to help with the baby. His big sister.'

And suddenly, without warning, her eyes filled with tears, which trickled slowly down her young face, and Refalo folded her in his arms, held her gently, soothed her. 'Would you like me to come with you? Would it make it easier?'

With a sniff and a gulp, she shook her head. 'No,' she said, her face still muffled against his chest. Taking a deep breath, she straightened. With another sniff, and after a frantic search for a hanky, she blew her nose, took a deep breath. 'No. I have to do it by myself, don't I?'

'Yes. I think that's best.'

'Will I be able to get a flight?'

'No,' he said with a faint smile. 'Not in the height of the tourist season. However,' he continued when she began to look panicky again, 'I can. We will go into Rabat, choose something for the baby, then we will take you to the airport, and I will have you flown home. Go and get ready; I'll make the arrangements.'

When he'd gone, Fran looked at Gillan and gave a watery smile. 'He's nice, isn't he?'

'Yes.'

'I didn't mean to be so awful.'

'I know,' Gillan said gently. 'Come on; let's go and get your bits packed up.' Putting a comforting arm round Fran's shoulder, she went upstairs with her, helped her collect her things. 'Will you let us know how you are, what the baby's like?'

'Shall I?' she asked hesitantly. 'Do you want me to?'

'Yes, very much.' With a smile, she began folding things that looked as though they needed throwing away.

'Gillan?'

'Mmm?'

'*Are* you going to marry him?'

Startled, she turned and said helplessly, 'I don't know.'

'They didn't like him, you know.'

'Who? Refalo?'

'No, my—father. They said he was a wastrel.'

Placing the top that she'd just folded into the bag, Gillan sat beside Fran on the bed and put her arm round her. 'There are lots of different sorts of people in the world, Francesca—the good and the bad, the selfish and the kind, the workers and the idle. Everyone has a good side, and everyone a bad. But isn't it always better to find the good?

'I think, from what Refalo said, that Nico was charming, happy—the sort of person who likes to make others smile. I don't know if he worked, I don't know if he was a wastrel, but wouldn't it be a gloomy old world if everyone was serious and industrious? Refalo liked him—loved him, I think—and if just one person loves you then you can't be all bad, can you?

'There is a need for people in this world just to make us smile. Maybe he *was* irresponsible, but he didn't know about you, didn't know he left your mother pregnant, and no one can say what he would have done if he had, so it isn't fair to judge. Whatever his faults or his weaknesses, part of him lives in you. Make it the good part, Fran,' she urged softly. 'The smiling, happy part. Don't judge a dead man by malicious tongues. He made you, so that wasn't so bad, was it?'

'No,' Fran whispered, her eyes filled with tears. 'Thank you.'

With a gentle squeeze, Gillan released her, found Refalo standing in the doorway watching them. Looking quickly away, she finished folding Fran's meagre bits and pieces.

'Ready?' he asked easily.

They both nodded.

'And if you want to come back,' he added quietly, 'ring the office; they'll get a message to me.'

'I can come back one day?'

'Of course. But don't come without warning,' he added with a smile. 'I'm not always here.'

And don't come with your mother, Gillan thought with a tiny smile.

They drove into Rabat, chose things for the baby, had them gift-wrapped, and drove back to Xlendi. The helicopter sat like a giant dragonfly at the back of the villa, waiting for them.

'We're going in the chopper?' Fran exclaimed in delight. 'Oh, wow.'

'I never knew what a capacity I had for pleasing children,' Refalo murmured drily as he helped them both in.

Not only children, she almost said, but he obviously knew what she was thinking, because he gave her a rather wicked smile. Blushing, she strapped herself in.

When they'd returned, and the helicopter was parked tidily on the small landing pad behind the villa, the pilot wandering off with a cheerful salute, Refalo smiled at her. A rather wolfish smile. 'Now,' he said, with a significance that alarmed her, 'a little privacy is called for.'

'Is it?' she queried weakly, with that churning in her stomach. 'Why?'

'Because I want to make love to you.'

'Oh.' Feeling weak and unsteady, not at all ready for this, she allowed him to tug her into the villa.

Closing the door behind him, he leaned back against it, drew her into the loose circle of his arms, stared down into her troubled face. 'You don't want to make love to me?'

'Yes. No. Oh, Refalo,' she groaned, 'I don't *know*.' And her body felt so hot, almost feverish as she stared back at him, allowed her eyes to linger on his mouth. A mouth that had already caused havoc.

'Lean your body against mine,' he ordered softly. 'Then kiss me.'

With a little snatched breath, a pain of almost overwhelming desire, she swallowed the dryness in her throat, stared up into his eyes. Such serious eyes. 'You don't sound very lover-like!' she exclaimed shakily.

'Don't I?'

'No. Refalo, I—'

'Lean against me,' he insisted. 'Kiss me.'

Feeling faint and shaky, she stared back at his mouth, felt the groan begin inside, and slowly, slowly moved so that their bodies touched. She took a snatched breath as they came into contact, felt heat spiral through her, stared desperately at his mouth, was almost able to taste how it would feel, what it would do to her.

'Just do it.'

Watching his mouth form the words was so—erotic, and she moistened her lips, let out a shaky breath as his mouth parted in anticipation of her kiss. Breathing erratic, heat spiralling from their touching bodies, she put up a shaky hand to touch his lower lip, then closed her eyes, slid both arms round his neck, and touched her mouth to his. Hesitantly, softly, her heart beating too fast, she touched her tongue to his. 'Don't just stand there,' she groaned. 'Do something. Move. *Help* me!'

'No,' he breathed, and her own breathing accelerated. 'Seduce me, Gillan,' he ordered even more softly. 'Arouse me.'

And that in itself was arousing. Feeling almost ill, almost supernaturally aware of the texture of his hair beneath her fingertips, the warmth of his neck, with her mouth barely touching his, his aroused body against hers, feeling the desperate fight not to press closer, and the utter need to do so, she slipped her hands to his chest, began slowly, shakily to undo the buttons of his shirt.

Moving her hands inside, she touched the warm flesh, scratched her nails ever so gently against his nipples until they hardened, and her mouth, without prompting, began to play with his. To touch, retreat, move—so warm, so soft, so good. And behind her closed lids were erotic pictures of what would be, how it would be.

Boneless and aching, she stood on tiptoe so that they fitted snugly together, and gasped at the contact. She moved her body against his, felt heat scorch through her, felt the hard muscles of his thighs, the belt that covered his flat stomach, felt her breasts flatten against him, felt as though her whole body was too sensitised, too aware.

'Refalo,' she pleaded almost inaudibly against his mouth.

'No.'

Oh, God. Releasing his mouth she leaned her head back a fraction so that she could see his face. His head was tilted forward slightly so that she could reach, his eyes closed, and she felt such an overwhelming feeling of desire, such a need for this enigmatic man.

Oh, Refalo, she pleaded silently as her hands moved to frame his exquisite face, allowing her fingers gently to touch his eyelashes which lay against his cheeks, black and soft as soot. She trailed them across his cheekbones, momentarily touched his arrogant nose, then went back down to his mouth—a mouth that kindled passion in her, so many yearnings. And as she slowly trailed one shaking finger across his mouth his eyes opened, captured her in their brilliant depths.

Her voice barely audible, she murmured gruffly, 'You look so serious.'

'Making love is a serious business. Isn't it?'

'Yes,' she agreed softly. 'But shouldn't it be fun too?'

'No.' And suddenly his voice was thick, husky, exciting her more. 'No,' he repeated, his eyes still holding hers. 'The first time isn't fun, it's frightening.'

'Frightening?'

'Yes. Frightening in its intensity.'

'But it's what you want?'

'Yes, Gillan, it's what I want.' And arms that had been loose, relaxed were tightening, drawing her closer until she could barely breathe. 'It's what I want.' Moving one strong hand up to her nape, he spread his fingers, held her head steady whilst he searched her face, examined every inch of it, stared deep into her wide grey eyes. 'I want you naked,' he stated with quiet intensity. 'Warm, pliant. I want you any way at all. Every way. Now.'

A jerked breath, a shudder, a liquid feeling inside. She couldn't speak, just held him, rested her face against his shoulder, and fought not to pass out. She felt as though she was going to, felt light-headed—and very pliant.

Taking slow, deep breaths, she finally managed unsteadily, 'Dear God, Refalo, but you have a way with words.'

'Yes. For three days I've watched long, naked legs, slick and shiny with salt water, sun, oil; I've watched a naked midriff, shoulders I've wanted to bite into, a bikini I've wanted to remove. And for three impossibly long, fraught days, because of Francesca, I have manfully refrained from touching you at all. Now I can touch you. Now I can no longer wait. And I can't reach your mouth.'

Blindly raising her head, eyes still closed, she waited for the affair to begin. Waited to be this man's lover. Wanted nothing else. Only this.

His mouth touched hers—and the phone rang, making her jump violently. Her eyes snapped open and she stared at him almost uncomprehendingly.

Ignoring it, face still serious, eyes still serious, he asked softly, 'You want this?'

Without thought, without care, she said simply, 'Yes.' And he smiled.

'Yes,' he agreed.

And the phone kept ringing.

It sounded urgent, as phones sometimes do.

'If you leave it,' she said raggedly, 'it will be important.'

'This is important,' he murmured thickly, 'and I've waited long enough.'

Holding his eyes, her mouth a hair's breadth from his, she worried. 'It isn't going to stop. And I can't make love to you with a phone ringing. It keeps intruding.'

'So it does,' he sighed. 'Don't go away.'

'No.'

'And don't forget where we got to.'

Moving her gently aside, he released her, walked into the hall to answer it.

Feeling wrung out, she leaned where he had leaned, put her head back against the door and closed her eyes. Her lover. Feeling suddenly cold, she gave a little shiver wrapped her arms around herself, and became aware of Refalo's voice raised in either anger or exasperation. That wasn't like Refalo; he rarely raised his voice. Opening her eyes, she strained to hear, and heard only the quiet replacing of the receiver.

'Is something wrong?' she asked with a frown when he walked back.

Obviously preoccupied, he stared at her as though he didn't even see her. 'That was one of Nerina's friends. Something's happened. I have to go.'

'She's ill?' she exclaimed worriedly as she straightened. 'Should I come with you?'

'No.' His own frown deepening, he said again, 'No, not ill. I'll see you later. I don't know how long I'll be.'

'All right. You'll let me know?'

'Yes,' he agreed absently. 'I'll let you know. Run to the restaurant whilst I pack a bag, will you? Tell the pilot I need him back.'

'This restaurant? The one on the corner?'

'Yes.'

With a nod, feeling bewildered and somehow neglected, she hurried off.

He didn't even kiss me goodbye, she thought sadly as she watched the helicopter lift away. An almost-lover. But was love involved? Trailing back inside, she absorbed the emptiness. And was this how it would always be—Nerina would call and he would run? Don't be selfish, Gillan, she told herself. No.

He was gone two days. Two days of worrying and waiting. He didn't phone. On the morning of the third day, she heard the familiar phut-phut of the helicopter and rushed out to greet him.

He looked tired, and unbelievably grim.

'Is she all right?' she asked anxiously.

He didn't answer, just brushed past her, dropped his bag on the floor and turned to face her.

'Refalo? *Tell* me!'

Staring at her, eyes like chips of ice, he examined her face as though he'd never seen it before. 'Tell you what?' he asked, and his voice was flat, distant, as it had been the first time they'd met.

CHAPTER SEVEN

'ABOUT Nerina! Is she all right?'

'No. It all went wrong, you see.'

'What did?' she asked in confusion.

'The plan.'

'*What* plan?'

'The plan you cooked up between you. The plan for her to stay in my house, to entertain—Mica.'

'Mica?' she repeated warily.

'I see the name is familiar to you. Mica. Real name Michael Kerrigan. A wastrel, a no-good, a man without compassion, integrity, morals. A man you introduced to her. A man she fell in love with because her *friend*,' he emphasised distastefully, 'could not possibly have allowed her to be with a man who was without honour.'

Staring at him, having expected tales of illness, injury, she was having trouble coming to terms with what he was saying. Needing to feel her way carefully, because she *did* know the name, she queried, 'She went to Sicily to be with Mica?'

He gave her an arctic nod.

'And she told you that I introduced them?'

'Yes.'

But she hadn't. She didn't even know him, only that he existed. 'What else did she say?'

'That he was a man who only wanted her for what he could get, a man who hurt her—as anyone with any sense, any compassion would have known he would. But you knew better, didn't you, Miss Hart? You conspired behind my back, allowed her to be hurt, humiliated.'

'No!'

'No?' he queried smoothly. 'Didn't you come out to Malta with the express purpose of deceiving me, my relations? Only, I came back from the States unexpectedly, didn't I? Ruined the plan. But you were already on your way and so Nerina was unable to warn you, could only leave cryptic messages.'

Staring at him, brows drawn into a frown, she shook her head in bewilderment. 'I don't know what you're talking about.'

'Don't you, Miss Hart? Oh, I think you do. I think you know very well what I'm talking about. About Mica being passed off as your friend, brother—whatever. It's quite unexceptional for my sister to be seen with my intended wife's friend, isn't it? No tongues will wag, no—'

'Intended wife? *What* intended wife? You didn't find out about that until after I'd arrived!'

He gave a mirthless smile. 'Didn't find out, no.'

'I didn't *mean* that! I meant—'

'That it was planned that way.'

'No!'

'Yes. After I'd been lulled into a false sense of security.'

'No!'

'No? A very nice false trail for me to follow, wasn't it—the story that she had invited you out for me? Which was so very believable because she *wanted* me to be happy, thought I had wasted too many years looking after her when I should have been out building my own emotional life. *Her* words, not mine. And, of course, Julia didn't get hold of the wrong end of the stick at all, did she? It was a stick Nerina had given her. No wonder you went to bed so quickly. No wonder you weren't angry; no wonder you didn't *flounce*.'

'*Refalo!*' she stormed in exasperation. 'I don't know what you're *talking* about!'

'And so the plan was altered,' he continued ruthlessly. 'Nerina arranged to meet him in Sicily instead, arranged for *another* friend to lend assistance in this illicit love affair!'

'It wasn't a love affair! He was someone she met, liked, fell in love with. It was never an *affair!*' she protested, 'And I didn't know anything about this! She merely asked me to come to Malta. Said it was urgent.' Oh, God. That was why it had been urgent. She'd needed Gillan as a foil. 'I didn't know,' she insisted.

'Don't lie.'

'I'm not lying!' Searching his face, searching for a sign of belief and finding none, she asked instead, 'What happened between them? Is she all right?'

'No, she is not all right. She's hurt and bewildered and frightened. She lied, told everyone you were to be my wife, deceived me and herself. And now she's been deceived by a man she thought herself to be in love with. She's *hurting*. As I am!'

'You wanted her to be young,' she pointed out quietly, 'play games.'

'Not with him,' he said distastefully. 'Not with a man with no morals, no prospects, no conscience. Not with a man old enough to be her father.'

'What? He isn't old—can't be old!' Nerina had never *said* he was old!

'Not to you, perhaps, but I would have thought even you would have considered thirty-eight too old for a nineteen-year-old girl. A very *young* nineteen-year-old girl. But you didn't care about that, did you? What did you care about, Miss Hart? A share in her wealth after Mica—' he spat the name '—had seduced her? Or was he intending to marry her?'

'No!'

'And so now you will play your part in minimising the damage done to her. *You* introduced them! *You* assisted in the deceit! *You* professed to be her friend, and so you will do as I say. Whatever she's done, she's suffered enough in her life, and if humiliation is something I can prevent then I will. If Mica is mentioned, by *anyone*, you will admit to knowing him, admit to whatever Nerina said about him.'

'And Mica?' she asked quietly.

'Has been dealt with.'

Yes, she could imagine.

'You will also continue with the fiction of our love affair. Everywhere I go, you will go, and not by look or action will you let it be known that everything is a lie. If I kiss you, you will respond. If I touch you, you will touch me back.'

'No. Ah. no. I can't do that. Not in anger and deceit.'

'Yes, Miss Hart. You can. And will,' he added grimly. Picking up his bag, he turned and walked out.

Slumping down at the kitchen table, she tried to think. Nerina had invited her, not for a holiday, not to take photographs, not for Refalo, but as a smokescreen. And Mica was old. Older than Refalo.

Shoving her hands impatiently through her hair, she gripped the strands tight, painfully. Nerina had lied. Had told her relatives that she and Refalo were engaged, were going to be married. Because then any friend of Gillan's would be unexceptional. But Mica wasn't a friend of hers. She'd never met him in her life. She only knew about him from Nerina's letters. And if she told Refalo, even supposing he believed her, what would that do to Nerina? She had lied to Refalo, and assumed, hoped that Gillan would go along with whatever was said. And now she, Gillan, was to be punished.

No. Not even for Nerina would she do that. They didn't need to tell the relatives, could keep it between themselves . . . but she couldn't allow herself to be humiliated, kissed, touched—not in anger and hatred. She couldn't do that. If he wanted her to leave, she would leave, would tell whatever story he liked . . .

She couldn't even think about the longer term, about a relationship that might have been; all she could think about was the *now*. She couldn't even really believe that their friendship was ended, because of course it wouldn't be. He'd spoken in anger and hurt. When he'd calmed down . . .

Hearing footsteps on the stairs, she stood, waited, then looked astonished when she heard the front door open. He wasn't even going to discuss it? Flinging her chair aside, she caught him on the front path.

'You're just going to walk out?' she demanded in disbelief.

He gave her a look of cool assessment. 'Yes, Miss Hart, I'm just going to walk out.'

'Without discussing it? You just fling a few accusations at my head and expect me to meekly accept them?'

'Yes.' With a look of dislike, he walked on.

'Refalo!' Hurrying after him, she grabbed his arm. 'Don't keep walking off!' Beginning to be as angry as he, she added pithily, 'And if you look at me like that everyone will *know* our engagement for the fiction it is!'

'How true,' he drawled savagely, and he pulled her to him and brutally kissed her. Releasing her, he gave a death's head smile. 'Excuse me, *darling*, I'm going out on the *Christina*.'

Her mouth a grim line, eyes narrowed in temper, she gritted, 'You aren't going anywhere until we've talked!'

'Don't give me orders.'

'Why? You give them to me! Ever since we met it's been one damned order after another. Do this, don't do that! Well, I'm not a child and I'm not an employee! *You* were the one who insisted I stay! *You* were the one who made all the advances! Never once did I have any say in anything! So don't turn around now and accuse me of inveigling you into...'

'Passion?' he asked distastefully.

Her mouth tight, pain in her eyes, she clenched her fists. 'Yes,' she agreed flatly. 'Passion. And seduction. And lies. But not mine. I'm extraordinarily fond of your sister,' she said harshly. 'I probably always will be. But I could have *loved* her brother,' she added emotively. 'And, as absurd as it now sounds, I thought, hoped he could have loved me back. But you didn't want my love, did you? You wanted an arrangement. A nice, safe, cosy little arrangement that would allow you to do as you pleased, behave as you pleased, continue ordering your life as you pleased. And Nerina's. And mine.

'Well, perhaps she doesn't want her life ordered any more; perhaps she chose to make her own mistakes. And, no matter how painful they are, she's the one who has to learn. I'm sorry she's been hurt, but it was no doing of mine. I knew nothing of her plans for you, or for me. I knew about Mica, yes, but only that she knew him! I never met him, never introduced them, knew only what she told me in her letters.

'And, as far as I was aware, I was only coming out for a few days' holiday! I certainly did not know Nerina had invited me "for" you! And it sounds just as damned stupid now as it did the first time you said it,' she muttered in disgust.

'I don't believe you,' he stated coldly.

'Don't you? Well, fine.' Turning on her heel, she stalked inside and up to her room. She'd already packed most of her things because she would have been leaving the following day anyway. So what was one day early? Slamming her case shut, she grabbed up her camera bag and stalked back to the front of the villa. Refalo still stood where she had left him.

'I'll take the car,' she stated abruptly. 'I'll leave it at the port.'

'Fine,' he agreed icily.

Her face set rigid with temper and self-disgust, she yanked open the rear door, flung her things inside, and slammed the door. Wrenching open the driver's door, she climbed behind the wheel. Firing the engine, still wound up, still angry, she lowered her window, glared out at him.

'And, whatever you may think of me, of my actions, my—morals, one thing you can be sure of, Refalo Micallef! I'm the last person on this earth who would ever do anything to hurt your sister. I, of all people, have very good reason to always wish her well! Because *I* was the one who supplied her bloody bone marrow!'

Shoving the car in gear, yanking off the brake, she took off, spraying gravel. Very good, Gillan, she scolded herself. Very, very good. How to keep secrets in one easy lesson! Now Nerina would know, and Nerina hadn't wanted to know, which was why Gillan had pretended to work for the trust, because she had wanted to meet Nerina, know what she was like, make sure, perhaps, that she was truly well.

A fine piece of meddling, she scolded herself. How very *altruistic*! Disgusted with herself, still angry and wound up, she hurled the little car round the bends very much in the manner in which Refalo had driven when he'd picked them up at the port what seemed like a lifetime ago. And it was very *satisfying*!

Still breathing heavily, face tight and set, she parked by one of the sheds, probably illegally, left the keys in the ignition, retrieved her luggage, and stalked off towards the ticket office.

'Miss Hart?'

Startled, she turned and found Cesare standing behind her.

'Oh, hello,' she greeted him lamely. 'Sorry—I didn't see you.'

He smiled. 'You are leaving us?'

'What? Oh, yes. I have to go home.'

He nodded. 'We will miss you.' Glancing beyond her, he frowned. 'Refalo is not with you?'

'No,' she said tightly. 'He had to—er—go out.'

'Ah,' he murmured with a wise nod. 'He went after all.'

'I'm sorry?'

'Refalo. You didn't want to go?'

'Go?' she echoed confusedly.

'To watch the sailing. Today is the Comino Regatta.'

'Oh, no. I have to catch the ferry.'

He gave a sly smile. 'And Refalo—he would not take you?'

'No,' she said, even more tightly. 'Would you excuse me? I have to get a ticket.' Dropping her case, she extended her hand, added quietly, 'It was nice to meet you.'

Patting her hand aside, he smiled kindly. 'We will meet again,' he said confidently. 'It is urgent that you go now?'

'Yes,' she lied.

He nodded, looked thoughtful. 'I can take you.'

'Take me?'

'I'm going across to Marfa.'

'Oh, well, that's very kind of you, but I can get the ferry.'

'Is another hour to wait.'

'Oh.' And in another hour... In another few minutes, Refalo could be hurtling down to intercept her, demanding to know what she'd meant about being Nerina's donor. 'Are you going now?'

He nodded.

'Then I'll come. Thank you.'

He smiled again, picked up her case and led the way towards the quayside and one of the beautiful fishing boats—yellow, blue, green, with tracings of red. A *luzzus*, Refalo had told her. With an impatient shake of her head, because she didn't want even to *think* about Refalo, she stared fixedly at the small wheelhouse that sat comically atop as though it had been an afterthought. Smiling vaguely at a young boy and a youth, who helped her courteously aboard, she barely listened to Cesare's introductions.

'Tobias, a nephew. And the little one—my grandson, Salvatore.'

With another mechanical smile, she sat obediently where indicated, her back against the wheelhouse, staring unseeingly as the engine rumbled into noisy life and the land slowly receded. Salvatore came to sit beside her, gave her a sweet smile. Dark hair, liquid brown eyes.

'I have to sit still,' he told her solemnly, 'and not get in the way, else I won't be able to come again.'

She smiled, nodded.

'I mustn't lean over the side, and I have to hold on tight, else I will have to wear a—a rein.'

'And you don't want to do that?'

He shook his head, grinned. 'I'm seven,' he told her proudly.

'And I'm a lot older.'

He laughed as though that was funny.

'I'm going to work for Refalo when I'm big,' he told her confidently.

'Are you? That will be nice.'

'Yes,' he agreed in satisfaction.

Make sure you get a contract, she nearly told him—something written down in black and white.

And as the land receded further she stared out across the channel towards Malta.

'Look!' Salvatore cried excitedly. 'The regatta!'

Staring where he pointed, she watched the yachts slowly disappear behind Comino. Any one of them could have been the *Christina*, although she didn't suppose it was. You couldn't just join a regatta, you had to be booked in or something, she thought vaguely; anyway, he was probably hotfooting it after her to demand an explanation of her hurled words. Or was he? Perhaps he didn't care.

Thinking of his yacht, remembering the evening they'd spent on board, she felt a pain, hard and sharp, inside. Perhaps she should have stayed, had it out with him properly, not rushed off in a burst of temper. Too late now. Anyway, it would never have worked, she tried to assure herself. Crazy even to have considered it.

But she had considered it, had thought of very little else whilst he'd been away, and now she would never know what he was like as a lover. Never know whether it would have led to something else. And he couldn't have cared for her very deeply, could he, if he could believe all that he'd said...? But then, Nerina was his beloved sister, and who would you believe, if not your sister?

She'd been vaguely aware for some time of another engine besides their own, had been gazing unseeingly at the motor launch that was heading towards them, but it wasn't until she heard Cesare curse, shout something, wrench the wheel hard over that she paid any attention.

Scrambling to her feet, one hand automatically reaching for Salvatore as he scrambled up beside her, she stared in astonishment, which only slowly turned to alarm, as the other boat didn't even attempt to turn aside. She could see activity on their deck, hear shouts, but it wasn't *real*—until they hit, and the world turned upside down.

CHAPTER EIGHT

AUTOMATIC reactions, instinct—Gillan didn't know what prompted her. She only knew that she grabbed the side of the boat with one hand and Salvatore's wrist with the other as the world tilted sideways, then hooked her leg round the wheelhouse doorway and hung on. Upside down, with the world turned on its axis, she stared down into Salvatore's wide, frightened eyes and tightened her grip on his wrist.

Someone, somewhere, was screaming.

Carefully moving her right leg up to join the left, she encountered resistance, squinted upwards, and saw to her horror that Cesare was wedged into the small space, unconscious. Blood was dripping down his face, pooling on a hunched shoulder. And if the boat shifted, even by a fraction, he would tumble out—and drown. There was no sign of Tobias.

Forcing down panic, with absolutely no idea why or how the boat could remain suspended on its stern without sinking, unable to see anything of the boat that hit them, able only to see Salvatore's frightened face and the deep blue sea below him, she eased her leg past Cesare's bulk, wedged her toes under what felt like pipes, and hung like a trapeze artist from the metal lip of the doorway.

Gingerly releasing her grip on the edge of the boat, so that she could give both hands to the boy, her voice distorted, she instructed, 'Grab my wrist. Do it!' she ordered urgently as she felt him begin to slip from fingers grown sweaty with fear. And when his small fingers had clenched weakly, she added, 'Now try and climb your way up me.' If she could wedge him into the wheelhouse before her strength went...

He swung with his other arm, nearly unbalanced her, managed to grab her forearm, and that was as far as he could go.

With a soft curse, she fastened her fingers on his small arm so that they were clasping each other wrist to wrist, released her other hand and managed to hook her fingers into his belt. Her heart beating like a trip-hammer, she hung grimly on.

So absurd, she kept thinking; so utterly absurd. Upside down on a boat poised to dive to God alone knew how many fathoms, a small boy dangling in her arms, his grandfather wedged... Her own fault. If she hadn't run away... And now she would die without seeing him again. No! He would come. Any minute now he would sail past, see them... Any minute now. He would know, feel something, telepathy... And, if not Refalo, someone would come...

The boat suddenly shifted, moved on the swell, and she froze, eyes wide, breath held at the accompanying splintering, groaning noise, and she prayed as she had never prayed before. Salvatore whimpered, and Cesare's arm flung sideways, hit her on the thigh. With a grunt of alarm, she carefully raised her head, saw that the older man was within an ace of tumbling free, and tried to wedge him with her knee, which put a further agonising strain on her calf muscles.

A warm wind ruffled her hair, caressed her hot face; an impossibly blue sea sent swells to rock them as the sun beat down unconcerned. Unreal. So unreal that she wanted to giggle, forced incipient hysteria down, focused on Salvatore's frightened face, locked her eyes with his, tried to smile.

She wanted very badly to tell him that it would be all right, but her voice had gone, hidden somewhere inside along with her fright. Her head felt swollen. A rapid pulse beat in her temple. Her arms were beginning to quiver with the strain, her legs to cramp as she gripped each muscle tight to keep herself from slipping; her knee braced awkwardly against Cesare's unconscious form, she didn't think she could hold on for much longer— but the alternative was to plunge headlong into the sea, taking Cesare and his grandson with her. Just a bit longer, she instructed herself; Refalo will come, and, if not Refalo, someone.

And someone did. Eventually. What felt like days later, when her head felt ready to explode, when she felt sick and dizzy and hurt so badly, they came. On the wings of angels. The regatta. Not only yachts, which bracketed the stricken craft, but the support boat, and the media boat with its television cameras. Not that she knew that then.

Barely conscious, barely aware as her fingers were unclenched and Salvatore was taken gently from her grasp, eyes closed, she felt herself lifted, gave a sob of pain and passed out as her knees were straightened, her arms restored to her sides.

Lying on the deck of the rescue boat, a blanket covering her, she knew nothing of the rescue of Tobias, hanging grimly onto an oil drum as he was swept away from the wreckage with a broken leg, nothing of the struggle to free Cesare, to recover the two young men who had been on the launch that hit them, nothing of the fast journey to Malta and the ride to the hospital. She had no knowledge of the television coverage of the regatta being interrupted to show the dramatic rescue.

When she did wake, with vague, disconnected memories of noise, people, urgency, she wished she hadn't.

Her tortured muscles felt on fire. With a soft groan, she slowly opened her eyes—and hastily closed them again, but it didn't shut out the impact of a diamond-bright gaze. Breath held, she could feel him waiting—just waiting—and felt that squirmy, frightened feeling in her tummy.

'Go away,' she mumbled.

'Is that what you really want?' he asked quietly.

Cautiously opening her eyes just a fraction, she stared at him. His hands were shoved into his trouser pockets, and his gaze was—unnerving.

'Don't look at me like that,' she whispered.

'Like what?'

'As though...'

'As though I want to climb into bed with you?'

'What?' she whispered in shock.

He smiled—an odd smile, not humorous, not baiting, but...sort of hurting. 'Don't ever do that again.'

'Do what?'

'Run off, get hurt, nearly die. I've spent the last few years of my life in hospitals—' Breaking off, he took a deep breath. 'Bone marrow?' he asked quietly.

Too late to retract, too late to lie. 'Yes.'

'Does Nerina know?'

She shook her head.

'Why?'

'She didn't want to. She said...'

'Yes?'

Feeling incredibly tired, tearful, disorientated, she explained, 'She said you had advised against it.'

He gave a bitter smile. 'And she always does as I say?'

Her eyes enormous in her wan face, Gillan said quietly, 'I'm sorry.'

'Sorry? For what? Saving her life?'

'No, for telling.'

'For telling,' he echoed sombrely. Still staring at her, his voice as flat as it had been that first day, he murmured, 'Passion that almost was, accusations, a near-death. I feel incredibly old. How do *you* feel?'

'Older.'

He smiled, then sobered. His eyes intent on hers—eyes that bewitched, muddled—he said quietly, 'Marry me.'

With the breath jerked from her lungs, eyes wide with shock, she whispered, 'What?'

His smile was crooked. 'I asked if you would marry me.'

Uncomprehending, throat dry, she echoed huskily, 'Marry you?'

'Yes.'

'Why? You don't like me. You were...didn't...' With a feeble shake of her head, a disjointed gesture, she repeated helplessly, 'Why?'

'Because I can't think of anything else,' he said simply. 'Because that's all that's on my mind. I've been standing here watching you sleep, and that's all I can think about. Silly, isn't it?'

'Silly? *Silly?*' Levering herself up on her elbows, then falling back with a groan, she slapped her hands frustratedly on the bedclothes. 'You're *never* silly!'

'Aren't I?' With another odd smile, he moved to perch on the edge of the bed, gently picked up one of her hands, held it warmly between his own, then slowly lifted it, touched his mouth to the knuckles. 'I can't go through this again. I really can't. You looked white and ill and bruised when they brought you in—so small in that bed, eyes too big for your face—'

'I was awake?' she queried with a frown.

'Briefly. And I couldn't say what I was feeling. Couldn't hold you as I wanted. People in and out every five minutes. I just wanted to get you home, have some privacy. They want to keep you in another night, and I selfishly don't want them to.'

Staring at him, feeling helpless and unreal, she latched onto details. '*Another* night? What do you mean, *another* night? I haven't been here one yet.'

He smiled. 'Yes, you have.'

'No, I haven't. The accident was this morning.'

He shook his head. 'The accident was yesterday.'

'Yesterday?' she repeated blankly. 'I've lost a *day*?'

'Mmm.' Smoothing his thumbs across the back of her hand in an almost absent gesture, his eyes still fixed on her frowning face, he continued softly, 'And, watching you sleep, I kept thinking about that moment in the kitchen. Holding you, kissing you, feeling your warmth.'

With that odd, sliding feeling in her tummy, almost mesmerised by his soft voice, she didn't know what to say, so kept silent. Just watched him in utter confusion.

'I have examined, thought about, remembered every single moment, every single exchange since I picked you up at the airport. Every gesture, every word. My feelings on the yacht when we lay beneath the stars, those few days relaxing with Francesca. The way you feel in my arms, the way your mouth moves under mine.'

Oh, God. Beginning to feel extraordinarily ill, hot, she whispered stupidly, 'You said that I was the first woman you'd relaxed with since Nerina was ill.'

'And you think any woman would have done as well? No. I'm not a child and I know enough women to know the difference between need and want, between sex and— love.'

'Love?' she breathed painfully.

'Yes. I don't want to let you go, lose you. I want— you. I want to *know* you. I look at you and I want to touch. I want all the things a man wants from a woman.

And I want a son. Your son. Our son. Or daughter,' he added with a quirky smile. 'Or twins, or a dog—anything that will be shared with you. I nearly lost you, and I—'

'I thought you would come,' she interrupted somewhat blankly. 'Any minute now, I kept thinking, you will sail past...' Reliving for a moment the full horror of it, she shuddered.

'But I did touch wood.'

He looked bewildered, as well he might.

'On the *Christina*. I thought, I might be dead tomorrow...' With a weak shake of her head, she sighed, then groaned. 'I hurt.'

'Yes,' he agreed sombrely. 'I—' Breaking off, he glanced irritatedly at the nurse as she bustled in.

'Out,' she ordered him softly. 'And don't scowl; you can come back in a minute.'

He stared at her, looked as though he was considering a pithy retort, then obviously changed his mind. With a wry smile, he released Gillan's hands and walked out. The nurse grinned. Gillan felt as though she'd wandered into the wrong play.

'Sore?' the nurse asked.

'What? Oh, yes.' And muddled, and odd. 'I feel a bit light-headed,' she murmured with a bewildered little frown. Marry?

'The sedative,' the nurse explained gently. 'It will wear off.'

'Yes. I thought I came in today.'

'No.' She smiled. 'Yesterday. Come on; let's sit you up, spruce you up a bit. It will make you feel better.'

Stacking the pillows behind Gillan's back, she helped her wash and clean her teeth, brushed her hair for her. 'Better?'

Gillan nodded, still bewildered, still feeling slightly spaced out. Marry?

'Some physiotherapy, gentle massage and you'll be fine. We're very proud of you,' she added softly, with a gentle pat on Gillan's hand.

'Proud?' Gillan asked in bewilderment.

'Yes. And now I'd better let your fiancé back in; he is not a patient man—but oh, those eyes!' she exclaimed with a little chuckle. 'A man with eyes like that could make you do almost anything.'

'Yes,' Gillan agreed faintly. Almost anything at all.

'And then there's the reporter,' the nurse added with a grin. 'And Cesare, *and* his grandson.'

Distracted, Gillan just stared at her. 'Reporter?' she queried weakly.

The nurse nodded, laughed at Gillan's bewilderment, and slipped out. Holding the door open, she allowed Refalo back in.

Staring at him, searching his face, Gillan looked quickly away from those bright, bright eyes, carefully smoothed the top sheet.

'Feeling better?' he asked gently.

'Yes. Refalo, I—'

'You could have died,' he said softly.

'Yes.' Then she remembered the others. How could she have forgotten? Flashing her eyes back to his, she asked urgently, 'Cesare? Salvatore?'

'Fine. They're waiting outside.'

And, almost afraid to ask, she whispered, 'Tobias?'

'Safe. Broken leg.' Walking further into the room, he rested his hands on the chair-back, fixed his eyes on her wan face. 'I think my heart stopped,' he stated quietly.

Startled, she glanced at him. 'What?'

'I borrowed a motor bike, chased after you, and was just in time to see you go off in Cesare's boat. I returned the bike, was just about to call up the chopper to take me across when George called me—'

'I never did get to meet George, did I?' she interrupted foolishly.

'No. He said—' Breaking off, he took a deep breath, then continued, 'He said Cesare had had an accident, to come quickly. So I did, followed him into his house— and there you were, hanging upside down, Salvatore gripped tight, Cesare's bloodstained arm hanging out of the wheelhouse, and I think my heart stopped.'

'There I was?' She frowned. 'What do you mean, there I was?'

'On television. The media boat covering the regatta got it all on film. Not the crash, just the aftermath.'

Unbelievably shocked, she exclaimed, 'It was on *television*?'

'Yes.'

'Everyone *saw*?'

'Yes.'

Horrified, she just stared at him.

'It worries you?' he asked in surprise.

'Of *course* it worries me! To think of everyone watching, seeing...' With a little shudder, she closed her eyes, took a deep, much needed breath.

Releasing the chair, he came to sit beside her once more, reached for her hands. 'Why? You saved their lives. And I wasn't there,' he added almost inaudibly.

'What?' Nervous with him being so close, she was having trouble following the conversation.

'I wasn't there,' he repeated. 'And you could all have died.'

'Yes,' she agreed unhappily. 'I couldn't save them, couldn't rescue them; I just hung on.'

He gave a brief, disbelieving laugh. 'You just hung on,' he echoed.

'Well, I couldn't let him go, could I?' she demanded tearfully. 'He was only seven!'

'Yes. Only seven.'

'I don't even know what *happened*,' she said fretfully. 'I remember a launch coming at us, the crash, but I don't know what happened, don't know why we didn't sink. And if the yachts hadn't been there—' Breaking off, she shuddered. If the yachts hadn't been there, they would probably have died. 'I couldn't have hung on much longer,' she confessed shamefully. 'I tried, but it was hurting—'

'Oh, dear God,' he exclaimed as he gripped her hands painfully tight, 'will you please just *stop*? You could have *died*!'

'I know that! And you're hurting me!'

Releasing his grip with contrite speed, he sighed. 'I'm sorry. Do you want me to go?'

'Go? No,' she said in bewilderment. 'I want to know what happened.'

Looking down, absently reaching for her hand again, he explained quietly, 'Two young lads hired a launch— too big for them, too powerful—and they weren't experienced sailors. Going too fast, enjoying the excitement, the thrill, they decided to go out and watch the regatta. The throttle locked, or the steering—I don't know all the details; it's still being investigated—and they rounded Comino, saw Cesare's boat in front of them, obviously panicked, cut the engine too late—and the force of the impact drove Cesare's boat up onto their bow. Holed, caught fast, you all hung suspended.'

'And the two lads?'

'One is in Intensive Care with head injuries, the other, unbelievably, unhurt. Shocked, hysterical, but uninjured.'

'Oh, God,' she sighed. Searching his face, not really seeing him, only seeing how it had been, she murmured mournfully, 'And all I could do was hook my legs round the wheelhouse doorway, wedge Cesare in and hang onto Salvatore. I couldn't see Tobias at all. Perhaps if I'd let go, held us all in the sea... But I was afraid Cesare would drown, and I didn't know if his grandson could swim... I didn't know what else to do,' she added quietly, as though she were somehow to blame.

'You think you didn't do enough?' he exclaimed in soft disbelief.

'What? Well, of course I didn't do enough! If the regatta hadn't been there, they would have died! Tobias would have died!' Seeing movement in the doorway, she looked up, found a strange man staring at her, and demanded blankly, 'Who are you?'

He smiled, edged further in. 'I heard raised voices,' he began placatingly.

'I didn't ask what you heard, I asked who you were!'

Refalo looked round and said with the weary acceptance of a man who'd had far too many interruptions of late, 'Reporter.'

'*Reporter?* Go *away*!' she wailed.

'I just wanted to know how you felt,' he murmured as he took another step inside.

'Mortified is how I feel! You took pictures of me hanging upside down and showed them on *television*!'

'Film, yes.'

'*Film?* You filmed it?'

'Well, yes.' Glancing at Refalo, he pulled a comical face. 'She *minds*?'

'Yes,' he agreed softly. 'She minds. She thinks she should have done more.'

'*More?*' he echoed in disbelief. '*More?*'

Looking from one to the other, she pleaded weakly, 'Go away.'

The reporter gave her a roguish smile. 'Can I quote you?'

'Quote what?'

'That you should have done more.'

Looking at Refalo for help, and finding none, she exploded faintly, 'Well, I don't know, do I?' Bewildered, alarmed, she snatched her hand from Refalo's hold, went to shove her hair back, and whimpered in pain. 'Go away,' she pleaded. 'I hurt.'

The reporter nodded, gave a sympathetic smile. Taking a flat package from his pocket, he tossed it onto the bed. 'Thought you might like to have a copy. I'll catch you later when you're feeling better.' With a nod at Refalo, he edged backwards, bumped into Cesare, who was hovering outside, grimaced an apology and went away.

Cesare stared at her, eyes worried, pleading; a large plaster covered one side of his forehead.

'Are you all right?'

'Yes,' she whispered. 'Are you?'

'Yes,' he agreed helplessly. 'Thank you.' His voice choked, he urged his grandson forward. The child still looked frightened, and carried a bunch of flowers nearly as large as himself.

Smiling at him, she crooked her finger to beckon him in. He came sheepishly, obviously rehearsed, and presented her with the flowers.

'Thank you,' he muttered awkwardly.

'You're welcome,' she said stupidly, then smiled. 'Perhaps we should both have had reins.'

He giggled, ran back to his grandfather, and they both backed out, quietly closed the door.

'Cesare's afraid of making a fool of himself,' Refalo commented softly. And when she looked at him he added, 'He's been very emotional. You saved his life and that of his grandson, and he doesn't know how to thank you.'

'He doesn't have to thank me,' she mumbled awkwardly.

'Yes, Gillan, he does. And I would like to get back to—'

'What's that?' she interrupted, with an urgency that was patently false, but she needed to change the subject, needed to distract herself from his proximity, and desperately needed to divert him from his earlier conversation, which he was obviously about to reintroduce. She wasn't ready for that yet, didn't know if she would *ever* be ready. Her face almost obscured by flowers, she continued to stare at the package on the bed. 'It looks like a video.'

He sighed, gave a very wry smile. 'It is. A video of the rescue. They thought you might like to see it.'

With a little shiver, she shook her head.

'Perhaps later?'

'Yes,' she agreed. 'Later,' and didn't see his smile.

Looking round for some other innocuous subject to discuss, she stared at a print on one wall, and suddenly stilled, her eyes wide with alarm. 'Oh, my God!' she exclaimed slowly. 'Tunisia.' Shoving the flowers to one side, thrusting back the covers, and before Refalo could stop her, she attempted to get out of bed, swayed, put her feet down to save herself, and yelped in pain.

'Gillan!' Refalo snapped in exasperation as he hurried round to the other side of the bed. 'What on earth do you think you're doing?'

But she wasn't listening; she was staring in horror at the angry red swellings that decorated her calves from knee to ankle. As though disbelieving of what she saw, she gingerly touched a finger to one. 'No *wonder* they hurt! Just *look* at them!'

He was. Perching on the edge of the bed beside her, he ordered quietly, 'Get back into bed.'

'No,' she refused absently as she continued to stare at her legs. 'I have to go to Tunisia.'

'No, you don't. The fashion shoot's been postponed.'

'What?' Swinging round, finding him too close, she edged nervously away, kept her eyes from his. 'Who said it's been postponed?'

'Harry someone-or-other.'

'Parker,' she supplied faintly.

'Yes. He rang my home, and when the phone isn't answered there it's switched to my office. They rang me just as I was about to follow you. If they hadn't, I would have caught you... And Cesare and his grandson would have died.'

As she stared at him, no suitable answer or comment came into her mind, and, unaware of the gaping hospital gown, she jumped when he gently rearranged it to cover her naked back.

'You find my touch so distasteful?' he asked quietly.

Snapping back to him, shocked, she exclaimed vehemently, 'No!' Unable to hold his gaze, she mumbled, 'You startled me, that's all.'

'And have been startling you ever since you woke?'

'Yes. No. Oh, Refalo,' she cried helplessly, 'I can't... don't...'

'Can't marry me? Don't want to marry me?' he asked gently.

'I don't *know*! How can you want to marry me? You *can't* want to marry someone you've known just over a week!'

'Can't I? Ever since that kiss on board the *Christina* I've wanted you for my wife. I've made a fortune by trusting my instincts, on quick judgements, gut feelings; I've never been wrong yet.'

'You didn't trust them when you came back from seeing Nerina.'

'No,' he sighed. 'I was rather foolishly hoping you'd forgotten that.'

'Well, I haven't. You wouldn't even let me explain!'

'No. She threw herself into my arms, sobbed, begged me to make it better—and I *hated* you for doing that to her.'

'But I didn't.'

'No,' he agreed, his blue eyes darker, reflective. 'And because I was angry and hurting and savage it nearly got you killed. You were Nerina's friend; you didn't owe me anything, didn't have to explain anything to me...'

With a twisted smile, he added, 'And I spouted some puerile rubbish about you being too old for her, about wanting her to learn on her own, grow up...' Glancing at her, he gave a sad smile. 'And so I took it out on you. You don't even hate me for it, do you?'

Glancing away, she shook her head. 'You were upset; it's only natural you should believe your sister over me.'

'So high-minded?' he asked softly.

With a little shrug, she murmured, 'Anyway, I shouldn't have run away, should have stayed and made you listen.'

'Should you? *Could* you have made me listen?'

'I don't know,' she mumbled. 'But if you'd cared for me you would at least have given me the benefit of the doubt.'

'No,' he said gently. 'Caring for you, I hurt too much to give you the benefit of the doubt. Until I'd calmed down. Until I saw you nearly die. It could work,' he tried to persuade her softly, mesmerisingly, as he trailed one finger down her cheek, making her shiver with awareness.

Yes, it could. On the other hand... 'I need time,' she murmured.

'No.'

'What?'

'No. No time. You're nearly thirty...'

'Refalo!'

He gave an unrepentant grin.

'You can't know if you love someone in such a short space of time,' she insisted.

'Yes, you can. You don't love me?'

'I don't *know*!' she exclaimed crossly. 'You affect me *profoundly*, but I don't know if it's love. Anyway, I'm ordinary. I didn't set out to—'

'Attract me? I know.'

'No, you don't. You said... And I only came out because Nerina asked me to, and to take photo...graphs...' she trailed off. 'Oh, my God. My cameras.'

Tempted to tell her they were at the bottom of the South Comina Channel, he soothed wryly, 'They're safe. They were hooked up on the wheelhouse. Didn't even get wet. Sadly, your suitcase wasn't quite so lucky.'

'You mean I have nothing to wear?'

He smiled—an odd smile, not humorous, not anything really, just a slight movement of his mouth. It was a mouth that had once promised passion—and could again. 'It was rescued, and don't keep shying away from me as though I were about to bite. I would *like* to bite,' he added with amusement, 'but I won't. Maria dashed over to help,' he continued in the same wry voice, 'comfort, do something for you, and found a soggy suitcase full of waterlogged clothes. She's washed them, ironed them, but she doesn't know if anything has shrunk.'

'Oh, that was kind of her.'

'Yes. She's fond of you. So, can we now—?' Breaking off again, he turned resignedly towards the door as it opened to admit the nurse.

'It's time for Miss Hart's physiotherapy,' she said brightly.

He looked at her, sighed, nodded, got reluctantly to his feet.

'And then it will be time for her dinner.'

His smile turned wryer.

'Come back at seven.'

He nodded, flapped his hand at Gillan and walked out. The nurse giggled.

Promptly at seven, he was back. Freshly showered, shaved, almost formal in well-fitting grey trousers and a blue shirt, he stood in the doorway watching her. 'I've come to take you home,' he said softly.

'Home?' she echoed stupidly.

'Yes,' he agreed. 'Home.'

'My home, do you mean?'

'No, mine.'

With that disturbing pain in the pit of her stomach, she just stared at him like a hypnotised rabbit, because his eyes promised—something.

'I don't have anything to wear.'

'Yes, you do.' Producing a small holdall from behind his back, he solemnly handed it to her.

Warily taking it, she put it on the bed, slowly unzipped it. New clothes, she discovered, and she looked at him in query. 'Mine shrank?'

He shook his head. 'I don't know—thought it best not to take a chance.'

'That was thoughtful,' she said quietly.

'Mmm. Sometimes I can be. Do you need any help to dress?'

'No!' she exclaimed, too quickly, and he smiled—a rather wolfish smile that promised more than... something.

'Then I'll leave you to change.'

She gave a helpless nod, felt breathless.

After dressing awkwardly in the long skirt that hid her bruised legs and struggling into a loose top, exhausted by the effort, she sank thankfully down onto the edge of the bed to wait.

On the short drive to his home, Refalo whistled softly under his breath, and Gillan sat in stiffly constrained silence. She was frightened, and she didn't know why. She wasn't afraid of him—only afraid of how he could affect her.

'Where are you going?' she asked in surprise when he drove past the car park where he'd parked before.

'No need to sound so alarmed,' he soothed, just the hint of a smile in his voice. 'To my home, I told you.'

'Then why aren't you parking in the car park? You said you couldn't drive to the house.'

'Special permission,' he said softly. 'For a heroine.'

'Don't,' she said awkwardly. 'Don't say that; it isn't true.'

'Isn't it?'

'No.'

Stopping outside the house, he helped her out, and found Maria waiting for them. A very emotional Maria. She hugged her, wiped her eyes, tried to usher her gently into the lounge as though she were fragile. Which she did indeed feel.

'No,' Refalo said softly as he halted their progress. 'She needs to rest.'

With that alarming dip in her stomach, she looked at him, opened her mouth to disagree, and he smiled, scooped her up as though she were a child, and carried her upstairs to the room she had occupied previously what felt like years ago.

He opened the door, carried her inside, and lay her gently on the bed.

Heart beating too fast, she stared warily up at him.

'Do you need anything?'

'No,' she croaked.

'Good.'

Returning to the door, he closed it, turned the key in the lock.

'We don't want to be disturbed, do we?'

Barely able to breathe, she managed, 'Why don't we?'

'Don't be obtuse, Gillan,' he scolded softly.

'Refalo...' she began warningly.

'Yes?' Treading softly over to the bed, he perched on the edge, trailed warm fingers down her cheek. 'Your breathing's a bit erratic,' he observed mockingly.

'I'm not well,' she muttered stupidly.

'I'll make you better,' he promised.

'No,' she said raggedly, and tried to slap his hand away as it moved from her cheek to her neck.

'Do you hate me?' he asked conversationally.

'No. I don't like you very much right at this moment,' she retorted bravely, 'but no, I don't hate you.'

'Good.' Moving his hand, he trailed it to beneath her breast, held it flat against her heart. 'Good strong beat.'

Grasping his wrist, she tried to move it away, and he smiled.

'Why do I make you so nervous?'

'You don't,' she denied quickly.

'Liar. Tell me about Nerina.'

'What?'

'Tell me about being a donor.'

Wary, relieved, still feeling stupidly panicky, and with an almost overwhelming desire to give in, reach out, touch him, smooth that thick hair back from his forehead, she swallowed, asked rather thickly, 'Does she know?'

'Nerina? Yes. I rang her when I came home to change.'

'What did she say?'

'It was more a case of what she didn't say. There was a shocked silence—' he smiled '—and then she said, in great haste, that she was on her way.'

'Here?'

'Mmm. Now tell me.'

'I don't know how much you know.'

'Not enough. I need to know the how, the when and the why. I knew of your letters, knew of your meeting. I came over to London with her but she said she wanted to meet you alone. I knew you were a volunteer at the trust.'

With a shaky sigh, wishing he would remove his hand, glad that he hadn't, she stared at the ceiling, said softly, 'No. I wasn't. That was a lie. I didn't work for the trust. I'd better start at the beginning, hadn't I?'

'Yes—always a good place to start.'

With a helpless sigh, she said, 'Five years ago a friend died of leukaemia. A bone-marrow transplant could, perhaps, have saved her, but a suitable donor couldn't be found. Because of that, I went on Britain's Bone Marrow Trust register. I filed my card and thought no more about it.

'And then, two years ago, there was a request for a further blood test. I had been asked to send a sample for more detailed testing once before, but nothing came of it, and I didn't expect it to this time. When they told me I was needed, that the transplant was on, I was almost paralysed with fear. Suppose I got ill, had an accident? Someone, somewhere, was relying on me. It felt such an awful responsibility.'

Remembering that day, how she had felt, her voice became softer and he had to strain to hear.

'All I was told was that it was for a young girl. I was given a thorough check-up, booked into a London clinic; two surgeons took the bone marrow under a general anaesthetic. It took a few hours. It didn't hurt, and, except for a couple of bruises on my back, that was it. I was a little bit stiff, but that wore off in a couple of days.

'I also knew that the people who arrange transplants observe a strict rule of silence about donors and patients. They insist on anonymity for up to a year afterwards.'

'Yes,' he agreed neutrally.

'I sent a get-well card, care of the trust,' she continued raggedly. 'I didn't say I was the donor, just wished her well. Nerina wrote back. And two months after her operation she wrote again. She said she didn't want to know who the donor was, that her brother had advised against it, but, if I didn't mind, could she write to me, that it was a help to write to someone who understood what she had been through.

'It was censored by the trust, of course, and any clues to her identity whited out. But I wanted to meet her, know her, because it felt...it felt as though she were part of me.' Glancing at him, then quickly away again, she whispered, 'Can you understand?'

'Yes,' he said quietly.

'And so I lied to her. It seemed such a harmless deception.' With a small, sad smile, she added, 'Every time I got a letter, I reached for the thinners and razor blades in an effort to find out more about her. I meant no harm, Refalo.'

'No,' he agreed.

No? Did he believe she hadn't meant harm? With another little sigh, she continued, 'And then, just under a year ago, the censoring stopped. Six months ago, we met for the first time.' Turning once more to stare up at him, her own face earnest, she added, 'I didn't want anything from her, just wanted to know what she was like. To meet her. That's *all*.'

He didn't answer, merely continued to wait.

'We met in the Dorchester, and we both cried. I didn't ask again if she wanted to know who the donor was, and she didn't mention it. I wasn't ever going to tell her. Or you,' she added softly.

'Only I made you angry.'

'Yes.'

'And she didn't ask because I had warned her against it. Supposing she didn't like whoever it was? Supposing they were—unsuitable?'

With a grim smile, she murmured, 'As I was.'

'No.'

'Yes. Too old for her. But that's how we became friends. We wrote to each other—oh, every week almost, and met again two months ago in Italy when I was there on a fashion shoot.'

'I didn't know that.'

'Didn't you?'

'No. She was staying with an aunt. She didn't mention seeing you.'

'Perhaps because she knew you disapproved of our friendship.'

'Maybe. Go on.'

With a sad smile, she continued, 'A few weeks later, she asked me to come to Malta. No, begged me to come. She'd mentioned Mica in her letters, how they'd met, said how wonderful he was, said she wanted me to meet him.' Taking a deep breath, she added, 'She also said that you were being st... That you wouldn't understand and please not to tell you if we ever met.'

'St...?' he queried bleakly. 'As in stuffy? Stupid?'

Ignoring him, refusing to explain, she continued, 'And in that last letter, she asked if I would perhaps care to take the photographs for your new tourist brochure, and that you would welcome me with open arms.'

'But the arms weren't open, because I didn't know.'

'No.'

'And you didn't know anything about clandestine meetings, about being engaged to me,' he stated quietly.

'No.'

He was silent for so long that she didn't think he was going to say anything more, and then he sighed, moved his hand to her waist as though the movement was absent, unconscious. But the warmth of his palm against her side set her heart beating erratically again, reminded her of other warmths, other touches.

'I thought we were friends,' he said quietly, 'that she loved me, trusted me, would tell me everything about her life. I never thought she would lie to me. That was what hurt.'

'Yes,' she agreed. 'But not from nastiness. She's growing up, and perhaps the sudden freedom of being well, being her own person went to her head a bit. And perhaps this Mica encouraged her, made it seem like a game, derided your protectiveness, made her defiant. I don't know; I only know that she isn't naturally devious, malicious.'

'No,' he agreed. 'And you always try to see the best in people, don't you?'

'Do I?' she asked in surprise.

'Yes. Do you remember a conversation you had with Francesca about Nico?'

'In the bedroom? When I looked up and found you watching?'

'Yes.'

'I didn't mean to be presumptuous,' she began by way of an apology, and he gently put his hand across her mouth to silence her.

'I think that was the nicest thing I had ever heard anyone say. It brought a lump to my throat, Gillan. I loved Nico. Loved him like a brother. I wasn't blind to his faults, but I don't think even I could have handled Francesca's distress in such a comforting way. I meant to thank you, and then circumstances intervened.

'But when Nerina was telling me about Mica I remembered that, and wondered how you could have been so criminally blind, how you could have found enough goodness in Mica that you would allow your friend to be duped. Only, of course, you didn't. You'd be the last person in the world to want to hurt her. We both owe you her life...'

'Oh, don't!' she begged. 'It could have been anyone. There are two hundred and fifty thousand people on the register—'

'But it wasn't anyone. It was you. And we both treated you as a convenience.'

'Oh, stop it!' she exclaimed as she tried to struggle upright. 'The hair-shirt doesn't suit you, Refalo! Whatever I did, or didn't do, I'm not a child. And I did lie.'

'Yes, but not for gain—and why are you trying to sit up? I like you lying down.' Pushing her gently flat, he moved his hand to the bed beside her, leaned across her, looked down into her face. 'You're quivering again.'

'I'm in despair,' she said theatrically, and his lips twitched.

'Shall I tell you why I like you?' he whispered wickedly.

'Please do,' she retorted tartly.

'Because you don't try to attract.'

'Thanks.'

He gave a small splutter of laughter. 'I didn't mean you don't try to make yourself attractive—'

'Try?' she put in pithily.

'I meant,' he continued determinedly, 'that you didn't try to attract *me*. Didn't use feminine wiles—'

'I haven't got any.'

He laughed again.

'And you thought I did,' she argued. 'When I was late out in the boat and you rescued me, you thought I slipped on purpose. Kissed me brutally.'

'As I'm going to now,' he murmured, slurringly soft. 'Only not brutally.'

'No.'

'Yes. I'm going to make love to you until you beg for mercy. Until you agree to marry me.'

'No.'

'Yes.' Bending his elbows, he brought his face close to hers, breathed softly on her mouth, brushed his lips against hers, felt her sharp intake of breath with satisfaction, and lowered himself the rest of the way, let his chest touch hers, just enough to feel her nipples harden against him, just enough to—arouse.

CHAPTER NINE

EYES closed, Gillan breathed in the scent of him, the warmth, and groaned, fluttered her hands up to touch his back, feel the hard muscle there, the power, slid them to his neck and held him closer.

'Refalo...'

'Shh.' Parting her mouth, he gently explored its shape, moved to her cheek, nose, eyes, explored their contours with exquisite care, returned to her mouth and began to kiss her properly, with slowly mounting passion.

Barely lifting his mouth to speak, he murmured thickly, 'I kissed you like this on the rescue boat.'

'What?' she mumbled dazedly.

'Too late to rescue you, I got to the dock in time to meet it.'

'What?'

'Before they'd even unloaded you, I climbed aboard, held you, kissed you like this, and you were sleepy, pliant, hurting. That's when I knew, despite what I'd said, despite what I thought, that I wasn't going to let you go. That you were mine.'

'What?'

'And if it had been me, what would you have felt, Gillan? If it had been me injured, hurting, what would you have felt?' Raising his head, he stared down at her warmly flushed face, the lips that were swollen from his kisses, the dazed expression in her wide grey eyes. 'Would you have walked away? *Could* you?'

Her eyes locked with his, she slowly shook her head.

'Why?' he asked softly.

'Because...'

'Because Nerina was right,' he completed for her, 'and we suit each other very well.' Whilst he'd been talking, his fingers had been busy undoing the buttons on the front of her shirt, and when the last button had been undone, the material parted, and warm fingers touched her nakedness, she gasped, looked hastily down.

'What are you doing?'

'Touching you.' And his voice was thicker, huskier. 'I want to make love to you. Now. I *ache*, Gillan.'

So did she. And the ache wasn't caused by her injuries.

She wasn't wearing a bra, and as he eased the shirt aside she gasped again, sucked in a deep breath, felt her nipples grow taut, stared at him almost fearfully.

'Let me love you,' he persuaded her softly, and his voice was deep, hypnotic—the sort of voice that could persuade you to do anything at all.

Carefully folding the shirt to each side, he stared down, and only by the tautness in his shoulders could she detect any emotion at all—that and his utter stillness.

'Refalo,' she whispered thickly, and he looked up, stared into her eyes—and smiled. It was a smile to break a stronger heart than hers—a smile that told her everything she needed to know.

Careful not to jar her back, prompt the pain from torn muscles, she carefully raised her hand, began to undo the buttons on his shirt. She slipped each one free with careful precision—and her hand barely shook, she noted. Barely shook at all. And when she had finished, parted the soft shirt as he had parted her own, she took a deep breath, urged him closer until flesh met flesh, until warmth absorbed warmth and his mouth touched hers once more, until warmth and touch were no longer enough.

He undressed first, slowly, unselfconsciously, eyes holding hers, and when he was naked he knelt on the bed, continued to hold her gaze as he undid her skirt, gently eased it free, then removed her panties. And as warm air explored her nakedness she shivered, gave a shuddery little sigh.

Smoothing his palm along her thigh, then her flat stomach and up to her ribs, he slowly lowered himself to lie beside her, pull her gently against his length, and they both shuddered at the contact.

'Marry me,' he insisted throatily.

Unable to resist, unable to think of anything she wanted more, needed more, her voice equally throaty, she nodded and said, 'All right.'

He smiled, and it comforted her to see that it was a little bit shaky, a little bit awry. 'I'll be gentle,' he promised softly.

'Please.'

'Will *you*?' And she gave a funny little chuckle, leaned warmly against him, felt the renewed touch of their aroused bodies, and gasped again.

'Now?' he asked thickly.

'Now,' she agreed. And he was gentle, so very gentle, and loving—so exquisitely tender that it brought tears to her eyes.

Unable to hold him as she wanted, yearned to, able to do very little but allow him to move with infinite pleasure, she revelled in sensations that threatened to destroy her sanity. She gasped, cried out, held him as best she could, and when they lay warm and satisfied, curled together like the lovers they now were, she pressed a kiss to his collarbone, licked the salt from his flesh, and smiled.

'So beautiful,' she said softly.

'Yes.'

'And I feel as though I've known you for ever.'

'You have known me for ever,' he said, a smile in his voice. 'We've experienced more things in a week than most people experience in a lifetime, if at all.'

'True. What happens now?'

'We get married, live our life.'

Leaning back, she stared up into his face. 'That sounds nice.'

'I am nice.'

'I know. And...'

'Yeah, yeah, yeah,' he agreed comically.

'The word is *yes*. Not yeah.'

'So it is.'

Staring at each other, they smiled.

'And do you know what else is going to happen?' she asked.

He shook his head, an amused glint in his eyes.

'Nerina is going to gloat. Endlessly, and for ever, ad infinitum. At the least opportunity, she will tell all how she brought us together, how it was her idea.'

'Mmm. Shall you mind?'

'No, but what I *will* mind is being left behind. So when you go on business trips,' she promised softly, 'or any sort of trip at all, I shall come with you.'

'Certainly you shall.'

'And you will wear your dark glasses.'

'Always.'

'Because I'm not having other women staring mesmerised into your eyes.'

'Like you did?'

'Yes, and look what happened to me. I *still* don't know why I'm doing this.'

'Yes, you do.'

'Do I?' she asked with a smile.

'Yes. You adore me.'

'Do I? Yes, I suppose I do.'

'Only suppose?' he teased.

'No. Not only suppose.'

EPILOGUE

Two weeks later, flushed and happy, *taller* in her high-heeled shoes, elegant in a long cream dress of Edwardian design, Gillan stared at the milling guests. The *multitude* of milling guests. They looked like a field of gaudy butterflies as they enjoyed the lavish reception.

Except for Refalo, Gillan thought with a smile. He looked like an exquisite dove—an impossibly bland one—as he threaded his elegant way between friends and relatives.

'You *do* love him, don't you?' Nerina asked anxiously from beside her.

Turning, she smiled at the younger girl. Of a similar height to Gillan, with thick dark hair and big brown eyes, she had a fragility about her, a vulnerability that touched the heart.

'Yes. Impossible as it seems after such a short time, I do love him. Heart and soul.'

'I was afraid...'

'That he'd been compromised?' Gillan teased gently. 'That he'd been forced into marrying me because of what you'd said?'

'Yes. But when I see you together, when you look at each other...' Her eyes momentarily filling with tears, Nerina gulped, added thickly, 'I thought that was what I had. Oh, Gillan, I made *such* a fool of myself.'

'No, you didn't,' she denied gently. 'You were made a fool *of*, and what you have to do now is put it behind you. Every time you start to think about him, about what happened, snap it out of your mind. Be ruthless with yourself. You're worth much more than that.'

'Am I?' Nerina asked sadly.

'Yes!'

'Even after what I did?'

'Yes! This is my wedding day and no one is allowed to be gloomy. That's an order.'

She gave a shy little grin. 'OK.'

'And I told Refalo that you would be smug! Don't, please, make me out to be a liar.'

Nerina chuckled. 'We-ell, I did *know* you'd be perfect for each other.'

'That's more like it!'

Staring into Gillan's face, she suddenly squeezed her hand. 'I wish I'd *known* all those months that you—'

'Shh. And if you're about to mouth some rubbish about me only remaining friends with you because of the transplant I shall smack you.'

She giggled. 'It seems funny that part of you is growing inside me.'

'Then make sure you take care of it. You aren't getting any more.'

They grinned at each other, exchanged a hug.

'Getting any more what?' Refalo asked softly from behind her as he moved Gillan's veil and dropped a gentle kiss on her exposed neck.

Turning, she smiled at him. 'Mind your own business. It's girl talk.'

'Ah.'

'And you can't make love to her *here*,' his sister informed him.

'No, no, no!' Gillan exclaimed, laughing, 'Don't challenge him! Don't you know it's *fatal* to tell him he can't do something?'

Searching both their faces, Nerina gave a slow smile, reached up to kiss her brother's cheek. 'I didn't tell him not to marry you.'

'No,' Gillan agreed as she smiled at her new husband, 'but you did make it possible for me to stay.'

'And I wish you wouldn't keep *looking* at each other like that!' Nerina implored, only half laughing.

'Else people will think we're in love?' Refalo asked softly, without taking his eyes away from his wife.

'Yes. No. It's *embarrassing*! Everyone's looking!'

'Good.' Impervious to his sister's embarrassment, impervious to everyone and everything, Refalo slid an arm round Gillan's waist, drew her against him and kissed her on the mouth.

With that squirmy, wonderful feeling in her tummy, she kissed him back. And when they had finished to their mutual satisfaction they turned to look at Nerina, who had gone a delightful shade of pink.

'When you *really* fall in love,' he told her gently, 'you will want *everyone* to know.'

'Will I?' she asked wistfully.

'Yes.' He smiled at her. Extending his other arm, he enfolded her against his side. 'I like your hair like that.'

Looking a little self-conscious, she put up a hand to touch the rather complicated topknot. 'I keep thinking it's going to fall down.'

'It won't.'

'And if *he* says it won't,' Gillan informed the younger girl with a grin, 'believe me, it *won't*. Go and flirt with all the nice young men,' she ordered. 'Have *fun*.'

They watched her walk away, saw a young man approach her with rather flattering speed, and then they were lost to view in the milling throng.

'A secret wedding?' she laughed softly.

He turned to smile down at her, so much *love* in his face. 'No, a much *publicised* wedding,' he corrected her. 'I wanted everyone to know how much I love you. *Everyone*,' he emphasised.

'I think you succeeded.' The church had been packed to capacity—aunts, uncles, cousins, friends of cousins—and those who had been unable to get in had stood outside. *Hundreds* of them.

'It looks like a society wedding,' she murmured, and *still* couldn't believe that it was she who stood beside the most sought-after bachelor on Malta. Ex-bachelor, she amended to herself with one of her quirky smiles—and if it looked just a little bit smug, who could blame her? And she, who normally hated being the centre of attention, was now the centre of a *multitude*. 'I didn't think it was *possible* to have so many relations.'

'Oh, it's possible.' He smiled. 'Just not recommended.'

Looking up at him, she reached on tiptoe and pressed a soft kiss to the corner of his mouth. 'I love you.'

His arm tightened, and those beautiful blue eyes darkened momentarily. 'I love you too. *So* much. Can we leave yet?'

'No,' she laughed. 'Did you see the card from Francesca?'

'Mmm, together with the picture of her baby brother. She seems happier.'

'You've spoken to her?'

'Mmm. I rang last week.'

She grinned. 'So did I.'

'Yet *more* family. As if I didn't have enough—and here comes George,' he added all in the same breath. 'Hello, George.'

George bowed. When he straightened, his pale blue eyes were full of merriment. 'This is the most frightful crush,' he informed them. 'I would have preferred something a little—smaller. Gillan, you look adorable.'

'Sophisticated?' she asked hopefully.

'No, adorable. And why on earth would you want to look sophisticated? Sophisticated women look as if they don't want to be crushed. Look, don't touch. *You* look as though you would be prepared for any merry romp going.'

'Heavens!' she exclaimed, laughing. 'No wonder the relatives disapprove.'

'The relatives, my dear young lady, are spitting nails. Apart from that lady in the puce hat,' he added in a worried tone as she began sailing majestically towards him. 'Who *is* she?'

'Gilda,' Refalo told him, straight-faced. 'A Dutch connection.'

'Widowed,' Gillan put in helpfully. And George, who was the most confirmed bachelor anyone had ever met, fled.

Laughing, they watched her run him down. 'She was nice,' Gillan murmured. 'She actually spoke *to* me.'

'As opposed to speaking *at* you?' he asked in amusement.

'Mmm. How long, do you think, before all your relatives actually acknowledge me?'

'You *want* them to?'

She smiled, looked up into his face, touched a finger to the lapel of his elegant jacket. 'What I *want*,' she began demurely, 'is to have you to myself.'

'Easily arranged.' Taking her by surprise, and everyone else, he gently scooped her up into his arms and began carrying her out.

There was a disconcerted mutter, a pad of urgent footsteps behind them, and he halted, turned his head— and smiled. Blandly.

'Enjoy yourselves,' he murmured. 'Eat, drink and be merry. Gillan, throw your bouquet.'

Checking to see where Nerina was, she tossed it overarm, watched it sail towards her sister-in-law, saw it plucked from the air by the lady in a puce hat. With a snort of laughter, a mischievous wave, she urged her new husband onwards.

'Where are we going?' she asked somewhat belatedly as he settled her in the gleaming limousine that was waiting outside.

'Anywhere there's a bed.' Pressing a swift kiss on her mouth, he climbed in beside her and indicated for the driver to move off. 'To the *Christina*? Want to go sailing? Just the two of us?'

'Yes, please.'

'Greek islands? The Balearics?'

'Whatever.'

He gave a slow smile. 'Shall you always be this accommodating?'

'Probably not. But right at this moment all I want is to be alone with you. To make love to you, have you make love to me. With no one to see us, no one to—intrude. Tomorrow can take care of itself.'

'Yes,' he agreed in that soft, seductive voice that so undermined her every resistance. 'Tomorrow can take care of itself. Take us to the yacht,' he instructed the driver.

'Where would we have gone if I hadn't wanted to go to the *Christina*?' she asked with teasing curiosity.

'To the *Christina*.' He smiled. 'Don't you know yet that I always get my own way?'

'It's what you wanted?'

'Yes.' His voice too low to be overheard, his mouth close to hers, he continued mesmerisingly, 'I want you to myself. Want to make love to you when we feel like it, where we feel like it, and how we feel like it. Day or night—at lunch, dinner, in the shower, in the bed.'

Her eyes holding his, her breath feathering his mouth, she added huskily, 'Or on deck, under the stars?'

'Is that what you'd like?'

'Yes,' she agreed thickly.

Raising his hand, his fingers gently touching her mouth, eyes so very bright, so very loving, he said softly, 'Then that's what you shall have. Tonight, under the stars, our naked bodies cooled by the soft breeze, we will make love. The second consummation of our very unsecret wedding.'

'Second?' she whispered.

'Yes. The first is going to be—somewhere else.'

With that wonderful, special feeling in her tummy, she gave a shaky smile. 'It is?'

'Mmm.'

'*Your* fantasy?'

'*My* fantasy,' he agreed. Moving his mouth to her ear, he told her what his fantasy was.

Drawing back, she stared at him in shock, then delight, her eyes brimful of laughter. 'Really?'

'Really.'

'And you haven't—er—done this with anyone else?'

His eyes amused, he shook his head.

A giggle started. She tried to smother it, and couldn't. Laughing helplessly, she wound her arms round his waist, rested her head on his shoulder, and gave in to her merriment. 'No wonder you wanted the privacy of your yacht.'

'Mmm.'

'How long before we get there?'

'Two minutes.'

'Make it one.'

His own eyes alight with laughter, he instructed the driver accordingly. 'One minute it is.'

Smiling at each other, they slowly kissed. A promise made.

MILLS & BOON®

Next Month's Romances

Each month you can choose from a wide variety of romance novels from Mills & Boon. Below are the new titles to look out for next month from the Presents and Enchanted series.

Presents™

SEDUCING THE ENEMY	Emma Darcy
WILDEST DREAMS	Carole Mortimer
A TYPICAL MALE!	Sally Wentworth
SETTLING THE SCORE	Sharon Kendrick
ACCIDENTAL MISTRESS	Cathy Williams
A HUSBAND FOR THE TAKING	Amanda Browning
BOOTS IN THE BEDROOM!	Alison Kelly
A MARRIAGE IN THE MAKING	Natalie Fox

Enchanted™

THE NINETY-DAY WIFE	Emma Goldrick
COURTING TROUBLE	Patricia Wilson
TWO-PARENT FAMILY	Patricia Knoll
BRIDE FOR HIRE	Jessica Hart
REBEL WITHOUT A BRIDE	Catherine Leigh
RACHEL'S CHILD	Jennifer Taylor
TEMPORARY TEXAN	Heather Allison
THIS MAN AND THIS WOMAN	Lucy Gordon

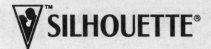

▼™ SILHOUETTE®

Tempting...Tantalising...Terrifying!

Strangers
in the night

Three spooky love stories in one compelling
volume by three masters of the genre:

Dark Journey by Anne Stuart
Catching Dreams by Chelsea Quinn Yarbro
Beyond Twilight by Maggie Shayne

Available: July 1997   Price: £4.99

☀ SUMMER SEARCH

How would you like to win a year's supply of Mills & Boon® books? Well you can and they're FREE! Simply complete the competition below and send it to us by 31st December 1997. The first five correct entries picked after the closing date will each win a year's subscription to the Mills & Boon series of their choice. What could be easier?

SPADE
SUNSHINE
PICNIC
BEACHBALL
SWIMMING
SUNBATHING
CLOUDLESS
FUN
TOWEL
SAND
HOLIDAY

W	Q	T	U	H	S	P	A	D	E	M	B
E	Q	R	U	O	T	T	K	I	U	I	E
N	B	G	H	L	H	G	O	D	W	K	A
I	I	O	A	I	N	E	S	W	Q	L	C
H	N	U	N	D	D	F	W	P	E	O	H
S	U	N	B	A	T	H	I	N	G	L	B
N	S	E	A	Y	F	C	M	D	A	R	A
U	B	P	K	A	N	D	M	N	U	T	L
S	E	N	L	I	Y	B	I	A	N	U	L
H	B	U	C	K	E	T	N	S	N	U	E
T	A	E	W	T	O	H	G	H	O	T	F
C	L	O	U	D	L	E	S	S	P	W	N

C7F

Please turn over for details of how to enter ☞

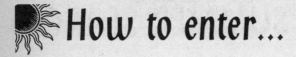 # How to enter...

Hidden in the grid are eleven different summer related words.
You'll find the list beside the word puzzle overleaf and they can
be read backwards, forwards, up, down and diagonally. As you
find each word, circle it or put a line through it. When you
have found all eleven, don't forget to fill in your name and
address in the space provided below and pop this page in an
envelope (you don't even need a stamp) and post it today.
Hurry competition ends 31st December 1997.

Mills & Boon Summer Search Competition
FREEPOST, Croydon, Surrey, CR9 3WZ
EIRE readers send competition to PO Box 4546, Dublin 24.

Please tick the series you would like to receive if you are a winner
Presents™ ❏   Enchanted™ ❏   Temptation® ❏
Medical Romance™ ❏   Historical Romance™ ❏

Are you a Reader Service™ Subscriber?   Yes ❏   No ❏

Ms/Mrs/Miss/Mr _____
                                              (BLOCK CAPS PLEASE)

Address _____

_____

_____ Postcode _____

(I am over 18 years of age)

One application per household. Competition open to residents of the UK
and Ireland only.
You may be mailed with other offers from other reputable companies as a
result of this application. If you would prefer not to receive such offers, please
tick box. ❏   C7F

Mills & Boon® is a registered trademark of
Harlequin Mills & Boon Limited.